HELD RANSOM

A Married People's Primer

Raymond E. Hartung

PublishAmerica
Baltimore

ISBN: 978-1-61546-971-0 (softcover)
ISBN: 978-1-4489-9001-6 (hardcover)
PUBLISHED BY PUBLISHAMERICA, LLLP
www.publishamerica.com
Baltimore

Printed in the United States of America

HELD RANSOM

A Married People's Primer

Prologue

Throughout time, human beings have tried to assimilate the various trials and errors that bedevil their existence. History tells us those efforts have only brought the noblest of societies to doom and shipwreck. This novel knocks on the door of several types of citizenry in a very personal way. The effort is an attempt to come to a rational understanding concerning the pitfalls that prey upon mankind. There are some lessons that can be mastered should the reader be so inclined, but in the main, this book hopes to entertain.

CHAPTER I

In the past, the Fourth-of-July had brought a sense of pride to a fun loving group of Irish people living on the eastern side of Tucson Arizona. That vibrant attitude gave the clannish couples the lucidity of well being. It was a much cherished feeling. It had been their goal as far back as they could remember. For some it had not happened soon enough. These former citizens of Ireland had, for a long time, sought freedom from stubborn English rule. Finally after years of embittered servitude escape came in the form of leaving their beloved Ireland for America. That new freedom became a law in several different forms. Hundreds of young Irish lads booked passage to America. They sailed across the ocean only to have a musket thrust into their hands. The inductees were given olive-drab uniforms and shipped off to a different foreign shore to die for a country that had yet to grant them citizenship. To the many who died in the process it was a noble undertaking.

Back before the turn of the century the potato crop in Ireland had failed. The persistent blight became a potato famine. In that fearful era the Irish did not have enough to eat. Mounting years of famine geared them to hardship: A hardship that outfitted them for the extremes that they would have to face in their new home.

Those who had the funds for their passage to the new world paid the heavy fare and crowded onto the faster ships even though they stunk of death. Hundreds of slower ships took weeks longer to find friendly harbors. It was common to find that one third of the travelers died on the way to America.

It was on these slower ships that the poor Irish were able to ascertain their futures while crossing the stormy Atlantic. The sickly ones swore they had made a mistake. The bloated bodies tossed overboard vindicated their judgement.

Boston was the port where almost every ship anchored, but Ellis Island came first. The very hardy Irish on board got to go ashore. Those who were ailing had their liberty put on hold by unthinking government administrators. That attitude simply added to their misery. In truth, a change of scenery might have saved a life or two.

Emaciated and generally ignorant of the ways of the new country, the almost penniless Irish became easy prey. For Ellis Island officials it was a way to plunder the excess wealth carried by the new arrivals. And so it was that several thousand citizens of the Ah Mick's left the verdant hills of Ireland. Prayer had done no good. Sunday after Sunday the priests in Irish churches rose to the altar and beseeched the Lord God for relief, but living conditions simply got worse. It was the beginning of a long struggle for the Irish population.

One enterprising preacher raised an ambitious thought in a Sabbath sermon, "It's a bit of a tale that I'm suggesting, and I've not been drinking too much beer. But listen. Perhaps this is a sign. It could be that this is God's way of telling our suffering Irish, that leaving Ireland is the right thing to do."

The response was overwhelming. Farmers and tradesmen

now found the excuse to depart the Bonnie Banks of their country, and by the hordes.

For them nothing could be worse than the life they were leaving behind. It was in that frame of mind that the men from Erin gladly went to their deaths. Dying for their new country as conscripts, or dying of sickness on the sea, their burial was the same. Stuffed in a sack cloth and tossed overboard, or entombed in a shallow grave, their missing presence was soon forgotten. The mental bitterness in life, and in what they saw in the new country, bore no resemblance to the land they had left. Either way, death was a witness to thousands of Irish emigres.

An editorial appeared Monday morning in the Weekly Post. One reporter for that major newspaper in Boston spoke out.

He artfully said, "In their final, heroic desperation, Irish immigrants won coveted respect for the nationality they represented. Many of those who cataloged the movement of foreigners landing on the shores of America vouched for the Irish as welcome members of this, their new home. There were other migrants who came from far off countries that faired much better, but because there were less of them their treatment met a better fate."

At the Fourth of July festivity, the jaunty, Irish summertime outing featured several games. Each presentation came with built in hearty laughter and honest fun. As usual, the celebration began early. Much of the entertainment was finished by the time the sun was past its zenith. The cool of early morning had long since been dispersed. The heat build-up came as an integral part of any July day.

The couples had planned to take in all the sunshine their bodies could handle. It would be the backdrop to fanning their happy mood.

The women planned to soak up the sun's rays from their neck

to their toes, hoping the look of robust health would last through the fall of the year. They all wore hats to cover their faces. Escaping from an accidental sun burn meant their light-colored skin would never acquire that leathery look.

The men dressed in shorts felt that a sun tan would enhance their masculinity. It was always this tan skin enticement that men believed drove the girls wild. Toward evening members of the picnic's suntan group began to complain. One man had developed third degree burns on both his shoulders. Luckily an older woman had brought some salve to combat the pain. She had a hunch it would come in handy. After she applied the salve, the relieved man graciously bowed and thanked the woman.

"I want to express my gratitude for the help that you rendered. I know it was not an act of mercy, but bringing the salve along was very thoughtful of you."

The woman's answer ripped the budding friendship to shreds, "If men had half a brain, they would consider the needs required for sunning yourself on the beach. As it is, you only bring yourselves."

Done in by the savage attack, the surprised man withdrew from the center of attention. He drifted toward the periphery of the party, grabbed a beer and melted into the crowd.

The center of the attention then turned to computer E-mails. The popularity of E-Mails became the lasting subject for the evening. Some Irish, computer Geeks allowed that they kept the better e-mails for redistribution at a later date. It was then that Ferggy, a crusty, older fellow spoke up.

Following that line of reasoning, he stated, "Creating a special folder, on the hard drive, gives people a specific place to store the best ones. Eventually I think the information will be passed around and copied. This Tuesday I received a copy of a patent concerning an automobile that did not use gasoline. Instead is used liquid nitrogen. The inventor claimed it would put an end to Global Warming. I did some checking, but got nowhere."

Some cat calls and a few snide remarks marked the answers to his solitary comment. He was trounced back by the adverse opinions of the crowd. Ferggy let the matter drop.

By now, the sun had begun to bow to the Western sky. Men and women began comparing suntans which went on until dusk. For some, the trending talks, about suntans, and other blabber carried on into the wee hours of the morning.

Most of the men had gotten so severely burned that the thought of making love to their wives never entered their minds. For the single men, foregoing a special, one time invitation was almost inconceivable. There were several men who swore their partners to secrecy for fear of being ridiculed.

This particular year was to be a special Fourth of July. It included a national celebration of rather gigantic proportions. In Tucson, everyone who had been invited to the picnic was looking forward to the eventful day.

More than three weeks in the month of June had gone into planning and preparation. It was the most ambitious undertaking the group had ever decided on. One gal described it as a gala: a joyous occasion honoring the brave souls who had made the trek to America. Most had found the freedom they held so dear, along with the patriotic laurels being prepared for and broadcast across the land. It was to be a much heralded tribute to the 400 years that came after the founding of America. America was still a country devoid of vile servitude and pernicious hate.

True brotherhood, at one time, existed in the breasts of every new citizen including the Irish. Collectively, America was in its heyday. Thousands of immigrants, from all over the world, spoke well of their adopted country.

Having sung the praises of their new land, they went to work each day, carving out their futures.

But old memories are slow to die: Almost all American immigrants had Irish parents or grandparents that knew the sting of English rule. In a steady measured beat the first settlers had laboriously raised the banner of freedom in an ever widening arc. Many of the Irish forefathers had found a way to overcome the differences that struck at the heart of the young country. Now, the wealth of the nation was in sight. Peace prevailed over much of the land, and the people who had come to America were overjoyed at their good fortune.

The clan, all Irish by birth, lived on the east end of the burgeoning city of Tucson. The land was less expensive, and a street called Houghton, where they had later built was the westernmost border of their neighborhood.

To be close to their homes, they intended to have their celebration at the near by park-playground. That city park lay east and north of Tucson, about a mile from Highway 10. Within view of most of the group, it was within walking distance. For weeks before the event, those involved in the planning met at numerous group meetings and rang up several hundred telephone calls. Many worked on the Irish costumes they were to bring, while others planned the foodstuffs and refreshments.

Weekly, they traveled back and forth between their homes and the park play ground staging each portion of the program with an exactitude befitting the celebration. Their wish was to be proud of their efforts. After the planning and preparation for the picnic was finished, the program's four man staff went over the balance of the remaining itinerary section by section. They found the agenda to be well thought out, a truly beguiling effort.

The gathering for the Fourth of July merrymaking had been numbered at eight couples. The group had received permission to hold the event in a roped off area of the public park. That area was well manicured, and it was not by accident. The ground was covered with a thick carpet of greenery. A small group of determined men, who had been invited to attend, had been watering the patch of grass for weeks.

The group leader offered this thought, "I want to make sure that the sod will be able to stand up to the hard usage it is going to receive."

Officially the male and female entries to the Fourth of July festivities required the wearing of the green. A sufficiently large patch of green coloring had to be prominently displayed somewhere on each person. If anyone failed to abide by the rule, a penalty would be levied.

Early Saturday morning, in joyous spirit, the party goers began to arrive. The gala included dancing, several games, a couple of kegs of beer, and of course a huge mountain of sandwiches.

Some of the games were set to begin right after the guests began to arrive. Much to surprise of everyone, Chela and her partner won the three-legged bag race. Laughter reverberated throughout the group when she came in as the front runner.

Margaret was the first to comment, "You might say that she is a bit on the heavy side." That innocent remark was enough to fuel the festivities for more than an hour. Soon after several other contests were started. No couples were outright winners in the rest of the contests.

Two of the men began to grumble about being hungry. They had been going heavy on the beer for over an hour. So, Margaret decided that it was time to dole out some turkey and ham sandwiches.

Pouring more alcoholic beverages came next which contributed largely to the loud gaiety. After the men had downed several beers, hilarity came to a full gallop.

The women were not far behind. After three large glasses of ale the ladies came up with a plan that would satisfy the men, and give the women a fond memory of the day. It was decided that a group pregnancy would honor the holiday in a way that none of the families would forget. The idea quickly took shape. The women were willing and of course the men wildly applauded the decision. The male conversation, with regard to the subject, went on at great lengths. There was nary a vote for refusal in the male grouping. Each female received a slap on the back, a signal to the women that all the men had accepted.

Not long after dark, the city put on a huge aerial fireworks display. In addition to skyrockets and pinwheels, other noise makers served to heighten the merriment. When the main battery of pyrotechnics began, the yelling, from the crowd, grew louder. A few of the revelers suggested it was because America was celebrating the country's quadruple centennials (The year was 1607.)

That part of America's struggle, written into history, captivated the party goers. No settlement of white people had managed to stay through the winter months until that year. The story was passed around on a printed sheet of paper. It spurred the assemblage's satisfaction no end. Feeling the need to add praise to the endeavor they all yelled and whistled. Everyone attending the picnic felt it was a timely observance of America's beginning.

Finally the aerial display began building in its intensity. Each timed skyrocket's salvo featured several different colored arrangements. Ohs and sharp yells could be heard up and down the tables.

Everyone felt the city had out did its self.

The last aerial bomb went off at 10:30. It was then that Martin spoke to his loving wife, suggesting they leave.

"Honey. It's getting late. I have to work tomorrow and you are going over to your mother's house in the morning to help her bake. I'm looking forward to some luscious, whole wheat bread. I hope you haven't forgotten. I'm going to stop by and beg for a slice of hot bread. A slice of delicious, homemade bread has been on my mind ever since you mentioned it."

Margaret defended herself.

"No, I haven't forgotten, but I'm having so much fun I hate to end the celebration. Tonight, dancing the Irish Reel, for the first time in years, was the crowning glory. I might add, that the band, hired by the city, was in excellent form. Martin, I've never before witnessed that many beginners out on the dance floor. Swinging all those smiling partners around the wooden dance floor made the men chuckle in glee. Their laughter made me laugh too. I laughed so hard I felt myself getting sick. The gaiety is infectious."

She paused to take a breath.

"I watched some of the younger couples fall down while they were dancing. Maybe they had too much to drink."

"Give them their due Margaret; the dance floor is quite slippery," Martin answered. "It could be the reason some of the couples fell."

"Yes, but it was fun watching them. I don't believe James ever danced before, but he did a good job of spinning Loretta around the floor. Her grins and her cackling put everyone in a tizzy."

Her husband added, "I'll say this. Well-being and romance were everywhere."

In the distance, a clock chimed the hour, and the band leader stopped the music. It was time for the band members to take their break. A funny quiet time reigned on the dance floor.

Martin started to praise his wife, "The core eight couples will never forget this Fourth of July. I have to thank you darling. You did a wonderful job in putting the party together. I'm sure it was no easy chore, and I doubt that it would have come off without you backing up all the details. It was a large bunch of people to oversee, what with all the different opinions and hangups closing in on you."

"Oh, it wasn't that bad. Privately, I did get some help. One bright, young woman, her name is Bridget, made the name tags. It was a chore that she did well. With the limited budget that she had, I have to give her accolades for her effort. Sharon, my neighbor down the block put the hats together. That really surprised me. Fortunately we had a few in the group who cared. I guess there's lots of help available if you holler loud enough."

Having said her piece, she poured what extra coffee was left into the trash can. A swirling soapy dishrag finished the job.

She again mentioned the volunteering group to her husband, "Pitching in, to help, is what it's all about. Some of the others offered, but by then I had plenty of willing bodies. I never counted noses, but several couples came by later to sweep the crumbs away. Let's see. That included Sharon and Sheldon, Bridget and Tom, Oscar, and the woman who lived on the West side. I believe it was Cleveland Street. Her name is Chela. Say, she's the one who won the bag race. Oh, and I shouldn't leave out Mary and her guy Peter. They were the last ones to show up, but they worked the hardest. I could have asked Lorraine and George, or Joyce and that tall fellow, Raymond, to stay and clean up. I know they would have all pitched in, but by then I had as much help as I needed. Of course, I thought it unwise to ask Eunice, or the man she had dragged here from her hometown. It surprises me that he made the flight. His round trip ticket must have set him back a couple hundred dollars. Gosh, I just realized that makes nine couples."

Martin spoke, "I asked Eunice about him; I believe his name is Tony. She said they went to school together. He dropped out of sight during high school. She doesn't know much about him, except that they bumped into each other in May when she went to visit her mother. They got to talking, and Eunice told him about the celebration. He asked if he could come. Ha, Eunice wasn't seeing anyone then, so she said yes. He's a good-looking fellow, and he dances well."

"She seems to like having him around. Do you think they could be serious about each other?"

"I think so. She pays lots of attention to him. I saw her go to the food table and bring him back a ham sandwich, some potato salad and another beer. I thought most men got their own?"

Martin interjected, "There's nothing wrong with being attentive to the man you're with, especially if you're serious. Countless women forget that men have feelings too. Sounds to me as though she's done her homework."

"I hope she hooks up with him," Margaret said. "She's always been reluctant to date anyone in town. Huh, that's not like the red head I know. You called her Penny, right? She dated half the men in Pima County, including you."

"Margaret. That was a long time ago. She was very young, and I was a dumb teenager. Months later I tried to make her understand what had to happen in order for us to continue being an item. She considered my explanation an insult. Three days after I spoke my piece, she sent me a two page letter. It arrived in the mail on Thursday. From the letter I found out the red head was carrying a great deal of anger in her heart. Boy, she was hot under the collar. Would you like to hear it?"

"How are you able to do that?"

"I made a recording. I did it with my computer."

"Sure, it's okay, if you don't mind."

"Penny really gives it to me, but if you're willing to listen I'll play it for you."

"Do you have it on tape?"

"As a matter of fact I brought it especially for you to listen to. I knew she'd be here today, so I wanted to make sure that you felt included in any thoughts that might cross your mind."

Martin shoved the tape into the car's cassette player and turned up the volume. The sound quality of the recording was poor, but the words being said were distinct and filled with emotion.

> I hate you because you're such an insensitive jerk. I hate how you treated me. When I tried to talk to you about our relationship, you turned your back to me and said nothing.
>
> You sat in your chair like Mr. Numb and act as though you could care less. That hurt, and made me very angry.
>
> You're so shut down, so distant, so damn snooty. That's why I'm furious. You make it so hard to talk you, and I'm sick of you blaming your problems on me, telling me it's because I'm so 'sensitive.'
>
> Listen, dear scum-bag, screw you. You wouldn't know sensitivity if it hit you in the face. When I came to you to share my feelings, you just tuned me out.
>
> It made me sick when you looked at me as though I was annoying you with my problems. Wake up, idiot. They were your problems too. It's because you didn't face them, that any chance for a relationship with me was out the door. Now maybe you'll feel something!
>
> It made me furious when I discovered you were upset because of what happened during the day. When I wanted help, by talking to you about it, you

said everything was fine. You're such a liar. You're so full of crap, and your ego is so big.

You walk around like some big macho bully, as if nothing affects you.

I answered her by saying, that's true.

I still remember how much we use to love each other. Is it possible that you could let me back into your life? Do you know how bad I felt when you hid from me, acting like I was the enemy or someone who would hurt you, like others have hurt you in the past? It tears me apart to lie in bed at night and feel like I am a stranger.

I cried and cried thinking about it. And yes, it made me sad, because I still miss you. It hurt when I reached out to you for a hug and a kiss and you shoved me away. Was I such a bad person?

It made me feel so unattractive and so undesirable. I felt sad and lonely when I saw other couples living with each other and enjoying it, being affectionate with each other. It hurt when I tried to talk to you about how I was feeling. You made me think I had no right to have a problem, and then you'd put me down again.

It hurt so much to feel you lashing out at me, instead of reaching out to comfort me. The little girl inside of me felt sad and all alone. I was afraid I wouldn't get through to you and we would lose each other. I was afraid we had grown so far apart, that nothing mattered anymore. I was so scared that you weren't attracted to me.

And still, you would not tell me. I was afraid, you wouldn't open up to me and let me in. I was afraid that you would rather be alone than work on our relationship. I was afraid that your old hurts had made it impossible for you to trust me and my love for you.

In my own way I tried to call you back. I left little notes, and sometimes, out of fear, I tried to talk to you, but in the end there was no way we could cross over the bridge. Even in failure, I was afraid you didn't know how much I loved you. I was afraid that we would keep on fighting and ruin everything.

I began to feel fearful that if I told you how I was really felt you would retreat even further into your shell. I was afraid we would go on fighting and never again be happy.

I was so scared. I used to sob for hours.

No matter how much I tried to show you my love you would push me away. More than anything I was scared, truly scared of losing you. I was afraid that we would never get back to the love we had. I was scared that no one would ever again love me the way I wanted to be loved. I was afraid I would wind up alone and miserable. I was so afraid there was something wrong with me.

Do I need too much love and attention? I don't know.

I'm frightened. Frightened—that you will read this and get angry instead of seeing me reaching out to what the two of us once had. I remember all the super-good times we enjoyed together, the trips, the parties, the home cooked meals. I'm afraid we may have lost those times of our being together. Afraid that if we keep growing and changing, we'll leave each other behind.

I'm sorry you feel harassed. I'm sorry I don't make it safe enough for you to trust me. I'm sorry I expected so much from you, and make you feel that no matter how much you tried to show your love, it was never enough.

I'm sorry I didn't always give you space to grow, and at your own speed. I know I pushed you and made you feel you weren't doing it right.

I'm sorry that you were so hurt by the past that you were afraid to count on me and to trust the future. I'm sorry that I brought such a needy heart into this relationship. I felt so rejected when you weren't there for me, when I needed you the most.

In all fairness, I'm sorry we fought. I understand how scary it was for you to talk about feelings. I understand how the little boy inside you was scared, scared of getting hurt. I'm sorry I wasn't more patient with you. I know that you were trying, and I know that you loved me, and didn't want to lose me.

I'm sorry you didn't always understand how much I cared about you.

I know you felt the financial pressure, and I'm sorry I didn't tell you more about how I felt. I'm sorry I didn't always ask you for what I wanted directly, and then blame you when you didn't give it to me. I'm sorry I expected you to be perfect when I was not. I'm sorry I got panicky when it seemed as though you weren't loving me every second of the day.

Darling, I wanted so much for us to be happy

together. I wanted you to trust me and trust in our love. I should have learned to be more caring, more patient, more understanding so you felt like you were not being berated. And yes, I wanted to be close like we once were. I wanted us to grow together, and to learn more every day.

I wanted to learn how to talk to you and not fight. I needed to know that you loved me as much as I loved you. I needed to have you hold me and to show that you needed me too. I needed to feel you would let me come back into your heart. I needed to know that you did want to work on our relationship, and that you didn't want to lose me. I wanted so much, to be happy forever, and have a great life with you.

I could promise to be more patient and not jump to conclusions. I could promise to tell you more about me and my inner child. But I also need to feel safe when sharing my feelings with you, and not be afraid that you will reject me or blame me. I wanted to feel close again, like we use to be.

I loved you so much, and I'm glad you were in my life.

I remember laying next to you and feeling your warmth, feeling you reach out and hold me.

I loved how you cared, how you pushed me to always do my best. I will never forget that. I loved it when you told me how proud you were of me, and I loved you for always being willing to read to me.

Thank you for having traveled with me this far down life's road. Thank you for growing with me, even though it was scary. I loved feeling close to you, touching you, and feeling like we could conquer anything as long as we were together. I wanted to grow old with you and look back at those hard times and laugh. I want to love you forever. You are my sweetheart.

I loved how you smelled and how you snored. I always knew you were there.

I loved it when you made me feel special. I know how you tried. Maybe we were growing too fast. I still like to think we could do anything we set our minds to do, if we tried, if we made a commitment.

I missed the feeling of you being my best friend. You were precious to me, and I wanted to be with you forever. Darling I just wanted to be in your heart. I'm sorry, if only we could have trusted our love and nurtured it.

I'll always remember how much I loved you and needed you in my life, needed to feel close to you, needed to hold you, kiss you, to feel safe, to feel like we were as one. To wake up every morning and see you and cherish you. Darling we've come so far, and yet I sense the end is near. Maybe, one day when the fires have cooled, when the pain has gone, we can rest by the side of life's road and tell each other what went wrong.

So my brave heart whatever the outcome, it was one hell of a ride.

Coming to the end, the tape machine shut down.

"That's the ending of two pages of anger and fear. I hope it wasn't too offensive."

"I must say she spits it all out. The gal does have a mind of her own now doesn't she."

"Yes, she does. In the three years when we were seeing each other I had even thought of marriage, but we never got along that well. Maybe we're both wiser now. We broke up when I found out she was seeing someone else. I got angry. So I started to do the same. That is when I called it quits. Margaret, I thought for your sake I should tell you my side of the story."

"It's okay by me. No one is perfect."

"Let me tell it as I remember."

Every light at Penny's house went out. An inky, ebony black quickly filled throughout the room. Rumbling, thunder storms crackled overhead. Lightning slammed into the ground, for a brief moment giving the appearance of daylight.

On a northern track, the violence of the storm moved closer: The wind's fury increasingly drove the gale toward the city. Rain battered the well-weathered sides of the main house. A small stream of dirty water leaked down along the edge of the wall. Near the back lot, the tool shed's old, wooden partitions shook, threatening further disaster.

I heard Penny jump to her feet. Fumbling in the dark surroundings, she found the green, Coleman lantern. Pulling up the lamp's glass chimney, she struck a match and lit the yellowish wick. At the base of the lantern, Penny twisted the key shaped, control-arm to the left, tuning the flame to a brighter glow. I felt better, more secure. Slowly the new, larger flame brought the corners of the huge rectangular, living room into view. Now that I was stable, I felt my self reconciled to the rampage outside the house. It sounded like the storm would go on all night.

I could hear the track of the clattering thunderstorm drive down into the long, narrow sweep of the valley. Ever more violent gusts of wind raced across the uneven terrain. Every man-made thing in the path of the storm bore the brunt. Even the trees bent to the fury of the storm. The wind's sound whistled an indefinable, morose tune, extending the intensity of my terror.

On the outskirts of town a power line ripped away from its moorings. Separated into two pieces, both halves fell to the rain soaked ground: One cable began a wild dance of twist and turn: The other section lay passive and unmoving. High voltage power, treated to a massive short circuit by the disjointed cable, played havoc with the electrical utility half a mile away. Several circuit breakers, heated beyond their capacity exploded.

Back and forth, catlike, I could see Penny pacing up and down the carpet. Her gait intensified. Then she found the middle of the dimly lit living room. There she stopped and tuned an ear. I watched fear pummel her senses. Her feature remained unmasked against the unrelenting wrath of the storm. The sneer washing across her face held me to a suspicion of her intentions. I began to think I had been used.

Above the noise, Penny yelled, "I can't remember a storm any worse than this." From across the room her eyes ogled me, waiting for an answer. Then, she tilted her head and closed both eyes. For a moment it seemed as though she had regained her self control. Opening them again, she revealed a cold, livid glare, that registered a compelling dislike. That look, ripped into me like cold steel. She was ready. The hammer was coming down. Penny's finger pointed at me. She waggled it to and fro. Then she directed it toward the floor. I watched her eyes turn to slits. Saliva collected at the corners of her mouth, coagulating in a thin, white coating. Drying spittle formed an oval around her lips. Screaming in an octave which seemed higher than Marion Anderson's highest note, she poured forth the brunt of her smoldering anger with loathing so odious I could almost feel the heat of her hate pouring out at me. I now knew for sure. Penny despised me.

Moving off, away from the middle of the room, she screamed

again, "What the hell's your beef? I never said Shawnee was heaven. Yet, you treat staying here like a sentence in some rotten prison. Is it really that bad?"

With a stride, she came back to the sofa. Carelessly she flung herself into one of the deep misshapen cushions. There, she started again.

"This is your shit, not mine. Early on, you knew I had a rap sheet. You knew it had more than one entry. You also knew, that exposing my legs had nothing to do with getting a suntan. Listen. You were also aware, when we got to know each other, that I had a crusade. Now I find that my personal conduct really turned you off."

I hadn't been able to say a word, but now I jumped in with both feet, "Penny, cut out the crap. I get shook up when you talk that way, and I won't stand for it. If you must spout off, take your pain and your ugly anger somewhere else. Damn, I've given this relationship my best shot. So screw it. If you want to kick someone's ass—go buy a dog."

I took a step forward. That one stride brought me close to where she was. I swallowed hard.

I won't get violent with you, Penny. That is not my style. I won't attack you, but I do want you to know I'm hurting. The pain from this argument has cut me like a knife. Our shouting at each other is wrong, and it's stupid. Can you understand that? Can you understand my feelings? Listen to me! You're not out in the world socializing with some Mam-Bee Pam-Bee Greenhorn. In case you've forgotten, I'm the son-of-a-bitch you begged to kiss. Don't you remember? It was the first night we met.

Penny cranked in an answer, "That's right. Yes I do remember."

"You bet you do. You're talking to number One."

That outburst was gutsy on my part, but I stayed with it.

"I remember, you slapped my face, and then leaned your body into mine like some girl in ripe heat."

I heaved a sigh and sounded off some more.

"You knew when you signed on, that you had gotten hold of an adult male."

"Oh sure. Ha, I was really impressed."

I puffed up and added another stinging remark, "If my small amount of griping is too harsh, you may as well forget about you and me."

Penny slowly raised an index finger, extending it in my direction.

In a tense, raspy voice, she said, "Fuck you. I don"t care about your moralizing, and I don't need your control. I'll do what I want, and I'll do it when I want to."

My temper kicked into high gear. I was boiling. For a spell, she stared at me, hard. She could tell I was almost out of control.

I did manage to save some of my self esteem by shouting, "If you'd care to argue the point some more, I'm willing."

Penny never said a word.

"I told you once before, the only way I can survive, is to be myself. It's what I've always tried to do, be myself. For three weeks, I've been riding along with your verbal punches. Hell, I thought you'd do the same, but no, that's not what you had in mind. Penny, if you're not willing to square this off, there's something radically wrong."

Now, I felt the hair on my back raise even higher. My self-respect rocked back on its heels. I had that eerie feeling of losing this discussion. It was not too far away. Somehow I knew I had to plod forward and hope I'd come in first.

"Penny, I won't bow to having a relationship with somebody, where guarding every fucking word I say becomes overly important. I'm not going to be constrained by some kind of verbal, strait jacket. That way, who can be carefree! That's simply idiotic. Is that how a person builds self esteem? I doubt that. I can tell you this. It's not for me. Yet, here we are screwing around with each other's heads. You've got some wild idea about saving people from themselves—better you pay attention to the people who count in your life."

The lantern sputtered, begging for fuel. In that last moment, the wick glowed bright-red. Then the lamp's use of kerosene ended. Pitch black, the room seemed to shrink in size. I watched the filament cool to a dull orange. Worrying about what might come next, I felt perspiration cruising down my hairline. I moved close to the wall not knowing what was about to happen. After my eyes adjusted to the darkness, I glanced around the room hoping to catch sight of her. Why was she so silent? Had she brought the 38 Police Special with her? I hadn't seen any bulge in her purse after she came back to the house. I took a chance, and looked around, but the gun was nowhere in sight.

"Penny—Penny, where the hell did, you go?"

"I'm here by the fireplace...the south wall, close to the window."

"You moved."

"Yeah, I guess so. Why, do I have to ask your permission to light a fire?"

"Look. I wasn't trying to make trouble. It just surprised me when you left the sofa."

"I got awfully stiff bending over building the first fire. It makes my legs cramp. Once in a while I have to get up and move around."

My eyes finally adjusted to the shadowy outline of the dining room. Dimly I could see her bending over the hearth. Having started a fire, she returned to the couch.

"Is our discussion over?"

"Hell no," Penny yelled emphatically, "You started this, but I've decided to finish it. I'll tell you once more. Everything you've said tonight is bullshit. What we've been talking about is nothing new, nothing different. It's all old business. You've paraded that same line of crap by me time after time. Sure, I use to suck it up like dry ground, but I'm wiser now. Get this into your thick head. I don't care, one good-god-damn, about your thoughts. Do you hear me? I only care about genuine feelings, especially my feelings. That is something you are not capable of understanding."

She bounced to her feet. "If you can't figure out what infuriates me, if you can't understand what makes me crazy, well then you might as well pack your bags. Your heading on out of here might be the right answer for both of us."

I began to sense the drift of what she was proposing. It scared me. I didn't want to leave. More especially I didn't want to leave her.

"You're thinking of getting rid of me? Why would you do that?" Her last sentence had hit me like a sledge hammer.

Penny, haven't I given you everything you've asked for? Sure, in some cases I've missed the mark, but look around. We have a lot of the things we need. I know I'm not perfect, but neither are you. As for my thoughts, the ones you just got through denigrating. In most cases they involve the two of us. When you whine and complain, you can bet my day will not go well. In fact, when you're unhappy, I feel terrible. Sure, I can take it, as long as you smile once in a while. What I can't stand is your hateful attitude. On top of that, you accuse me, no you blame me for your failures. Hell, I have trouble running my own life. Wedging my nose into your business is not for me. Right now you're suggesting I'm unhappy. That's not true. When I'm here, with you, I feel genuinely uplifted, even cheerful, glad to be alive. That means a hell of a lot to me. Do you get my point? You're an enigma, but I still think the world of you.

At the end of the sentence, I backed away.

You say I don't care, but telling me you're angry because the city fathers refuse to help nettles' me. They should support funding your project. Socially it's a good program. However, I hope you don't believe for one moment that blinking your eyes will bring them around? In this town, it doesn't happen that way.

Obviously my compliments seemed to sink in.

Penny, I'm proud of you. Starting a 'Center for Recovering Female Convicts' is a super idea. Stick with it, but realize your resources are less than adequate. How are you going to make the government listen to you? Fat chance! Petitioning private capital and businesses, for a handout is fine, but asking for government aid is passe. Congress is in no mood to continue funding giveaway programs. I'm telling you this. The heyday for a federal-dole will fall on deaf ears.

"Listen. I told you before, I don't give a damn what you think. Once, I felt like every word you uttered had some grounding in truth. Now, I know you slant these discussions in a particular way. I'll ask you, is having your way that important? If it is, it doesn't set well with this gal. It shows me how much you really care."

Her long agile fingers reached for a joint. I waited for the marijuana to hit and gradually adjust her thought patterns. It generally took three minutes to calm her down. It never came!

"For a fact, you don't care if I'm right or wrong. You don't care if I ever collect a dime for CRC."

Coming to the sofa, she fought against the press of tears. Flopping down on the same cushion, she dropped her head into the palms of her hands. I could see her grief take over, and grow. I watched the cigarette smoke add to the stain on her fingers which were already a dark tan. She was completely absorbed in self pity. Her body continued to shake. Penny took a last drag from the reefer, and then squashed it in the ash tray.

Glancing out from between her fingers, she seemed to be following the stream of dirty soiled water hurrying across the floor. The heavy concentrations of rain had forced portions of the porous, roof area to collapse. Sloshing through the narrow ruptures, water rivulets spanked the grey tile floor in the noisy pattern of a small stream. The repetitious din pounded at my sanity, but somehow the hollow sounding, plopping noise made me focus on Penny. The woman unnerved me.

It was now eleven o'clock. Frankly, we'd been at it for the better part of three hours. At that moment I didn't care about our future. I didn't recollect how the argument started. In disbelief I simply stared at her and tried to remember.

Penny, red haired, tall and leggy, liked to pound on a joint toward the end of the day, and now was the right time. Shuddering openly, her composure gone, she reached into a baggy, blue purse and hauled out the makings for another smoke. Her eyes were still glassy from the last cigarette. I stared, partly out of a fixation, but more so because of my interest in the deft movement of her fingers. Her habit of rolling the cylinder into an oval with one hand fascinated me.

It was at the Cajun Bar, in Shawnee, Kansas where I saw her doing that routine for the first time. Our get-together's had begun during the band's music tour, just outside of Kansas City, in more than an ordinary fashion. She had the hots.

I didn't mind her forward approach at all. It had been awhile.

Shawnee, as a city, had the usual, high, elm lined, main drag, highlighting the center of the shopping district. The bowed limbs formed an archway which alone more than satisfied the town's elders.

As for the younger set, it was the Hills Roller Rink. For short, they called it the 'Hangout.' Every night, the Hangout was the place to be seen. The Hills Roller Rink doesn't stand there anymore, on the little half street, back of the filling station. The October 1942 fire took it down to the foundation. Funny, a couple of months before, at the back of the roller rink, Penny and I had our first kiss. I guess you could say our affair had began then and there.

The last house on Main Street had proffered Penny a birth place. Ram shackled, to say the least, the house however suited both of us: For her, the building's familiarity made her feel quite comfortable. For me, proximity to central Shawnee, where the band rehearsed, offered the necessary inducement. My feelings were not a part of my decision. The small, 'back-door-place' where we made our music was less than a block away.

The home was sparely furnished. After several days, we went shopping together for staples. Later we bought enough furniture to turn the house into a decent, livable home. I liked the fact that her place was convenient to the town square. Located close to my room, at the motel, I, would sometimes stay at her place bit late. Sometimes, I even stayed overnight. Being that close and comfortable, Penny's place worked easily into my schedule. I made it home base. The money saved by quitting the motel took care of expenses.

At nineteen, she showed a well-proportioned torso. Blessed with the typical, strong frame of a farm girl, additionally she displayed a pair of emerald-green eyes; eyes that made one take a second look. With that haunting glance and her carrot colored red hair, she was, as the boys described her, a real knockout.

Hardy, her ersatz boyfriend, promised to beat the tar out of any fellow who tried to come between them. His feelings and his jealousy bordered on being one sided. Penny's friendship, although of long standing had never tipped her hand in his favor.

She allowed him to be in her presence, more as a kindness than as a beau. That was before I arrived. That was before she heard me make my Fender guitar squeal. I'll say it once. Hardy was no match for a guitar playing City Slicker from Kansas City.

Lately, he had been hanging around the roller rink watching the two of us. I knew he was angry. I was cutting in on his territory. It didn't matter. I thought I could handle it. That was a mistake. I hadn't allowed for a sharp shooter taking aim at the likes of me.

The five-piece-combo, I toured with, played several jerk water towns bordering larger metropolises. The band traveled Thursday, and played Friday and Saturday nights. On every occasion we pumped out our brand of loud Country and Western Music. Our main stamping grounds were small taverns, night clubs and dance halls, all over the state. The sizeable crowds that followed us propped up our popularity. Playing gigs from neighboring cities kept us busy. Financially, it worked out well. Every performance netted the combo two hundred apiece. In those days it was a good 'hunk of change.' You had to go hard, to spend it all in one night.

Before I met Penny, seldom, if ever, did I leave a new town without giving some part of my funds to the local, tightly dressed women of the night. It was a type of healthy exertion that left me feeling loose, ready to play music.

When the band first anchored in Kansas City, the yen for physical activity with the opposite sex had crossed my mind several times. I had been without a woman way too long. By two, I had ended an afternoon's practice effort with the band. We were all in sync. This led me to the Hills Roller Rink in Shawnee. I ambled over to the 'Hangout' and rented some wheels. In my day, I had become quite good at spinning around an indoor roller-rink. I had even thought of becoming a professional. That was long ago. Now nearly thirty, I was too old.

Soon after purchasing a ticket, for the matinee, I noticed eleven people were already there. Skating in such an atmosphere allowed everyone to show off their best moves. Of course, I began to perform. I skated backwards, did twirls and electrified all those present. Midway through my rendition of professionalism, Penny walked in dressed in a short, black, tight fitting skirt. Never before had I been struck so hard by the looks of a woman. I have to say Penny was the first woman who tipped my hat.

Strategically, she took a seat near the main door which was ten strides from the bathrooms. I almost lost it, watching her long, slim legs coil and uncoil about themselves. Here was a babe that could make you sit up and take notice. She had it all. The trouble was, she knew it. Hadn't her so-called boyfriend, Hardy, lent credence to that feeling?

Watching as Penny's eyes played over the skaters, grouped in twos and threes, offered a clue to her intent. Primarily, I figured she was sorting out the social areas that might require contact.

It was her day. I knew she could feel the swelling in her breasts.

Toward five o'clock, Milly skated by and waved at Penny.

Then, Sophia stopped to talk. The short chat produced a smile: Penny promptly displayed the appropriate gesture by turning a thumb down. Laughing, Sophia skated back to the rink area. Of course, as expected, Milly worked the men's bathroom. Most times the guys hung around there. Lean pickings, but Milly left no choice to chance. For her, being choosy was not a luxury she could afford.

By six o'clock, Penny had managed to corral several young bucks. Once they knew she was there—and interested, every male that she smiled at moved to where she had stationed herself. By the time I finished my special rendition, the semicircle of eager teenagers stood two deep. I stayed away. I had to take care of other chores.

Having left Schieffs' Little City in a hurry, I had not taken proper care of my instrument. Now was a good time. I finished cleaning out the case, and put the guitar inside. Tossing the ivory pick in on top of the Fender, I closed the cover and started walking toward her. From where I was, I had to take five steps to get to Penny. At the end of four, hearing the blasting report of a gun, I fancied for a moment that I could see a lead slug racing toward me. Anybody knows that's bull. You don't see a slug racing toward you. The velocity, being close to three thousand feet per second, made the speeding bullet impossible to see

Hardy fired only once. The dumdum slug squashed into my chest, and ripped out my back taking a part of my aorta. I didn't even have time to curse.

It wasn't easy to bury me. Caskets that fit tall guys are not stock items. The factory, out east, had to ship one in from New Jersey. However, it did give me a chance to report to my new, other world address.

For the few minutes I was there, they treated me fine. It was far better than the treatment I had been receiving on earth.

The next day, I had the itch to return in time to see myself lowered into the ground. I was shocked by the number of people that had assembled near the grave-site. I viewed it with a sense of gut enjoyment. Funny too, I wound up standing in the midst of the group, unseen, collecting the peer groups verbally, abusive words. That gave me a chance to notice who cared for me, and who had been fooling with my head all along.

Hearing Judge Key's eulogy, I took an instant dislike to the man. Taking fifteen minutes to expressly slap a fellow on the back for just living, gets boring.

Of course, Penny was not present for the funeral.

In her state of mind, I had not expected her to be there. The last time we had spoken, there was still a bitterness in her voice.

After everyone had gone, after the cemetery crew had heaped the smelly, dank earth over my casket, there was still one surprise. I never would have guessed. Looking back at my grave, I saw Penny. Squatting down, close to the ground, she was sending a dark, yellowed stream of urine arching toward my grave, urinating on that slight mound of freshly turned dirt.

Hardy never got the girl. The poky had his body for 20 years. Penny, huh, well it seems she married the town snip. A saucy guy, he handed her three kids in three years.

"Yes, she learned to cook, and that's the end of the tale. I added the last eight paragraphs. They are not true, but it finishes the story in a nice way."

"Well that was certainly a bag full of goodies. I'm pleased with the outcome. Your view point makes a difference."

Martin snickered and changed the subject, "Say, what about Tony and Eunice? I noticed she is sticking close to her guy. I know she's not a part of the group, but still, they do make a pleasing couple."

"Yes, they are a beautiful couple."

"I wonder who invited them?"

"I didn't invite either one of them."

"Then, why did they show up?"

"Leave it alone. They're not causing any trouble." Martin let the conversation hang for a moment.

"Oh by the way, thanks for reminding me about my past sins. I should have known you'd keep an accounting of my past." Both of them smiled, than laughed approvingly of the interplay.

Martin and his wife Margaret waved goodbye to the people on the dance floor. They again squeezed into their car. When the engine whirred to life, Martin turned the car into the right-hand traffic lane and started down the street.

About a mile from the picnic area Margaret interjected a new thought, "We have to go back. I forgot to take my baking tins. They'll get lost if I don't get them now."

Martin spun the car around in the middle of the block. Before he could get back up to speed, a siren sounded just behind them. There was no way that Martin or his wife could talk their way out of the ticket. The officer called it reckless driving.

The patrolman raised his hand, "Listen. I'm letting you off. I can smell liquor on your breath. Would you rather have a D.U.I. charge, or do you want to accept the ticket I've written?"

Martin gulped, "I'm sorry. I'll take the ticket as written. This is the first traffic ticket I've ever been given. I'm a bit of a novice when it comes to traffic violations. I thought you as the driver had a right to contest the charge. Apparently I was wrong. I'll take what is coming to me, and no crying."

He did not move the car until the officer was out of sight. Then he looked at his wife and scowled.

"You could have driven to the end of the block. We're not in that much of a hurry."

"You're right. It was a stupid mistake on my part."

Back at the picnic the crowd was stirring nervously. The music had started again. Martin noticed Eunice and her beau whirling about on the dance floor.

"Hmm, I wonder why Tony came so far? I'm bet it was for more than the fireworks."

Margaret added her thoughts to Martin's, "I think Tony wants to stay in town. After the big doings most everyone goes back to work. He came early, and he's staying late. Hasn't he been here for three or four weeks?"

"Yes, I think it's all of that. Anyway he's still here, hanging around. I know it's been quite a while."

She closed the cover on the container, and placed the large box of baking tins in the back seat of the car.

"He must have a job that allows him to take time off. I didn't follow the conversation that closely, but I think he intends to tie the knot with Eunice. I thought he was ready to ask her here at the picnic party."

Penny and her escort, ambled over to where Eunice was standing. She embellished Margaret's parting words with those of her own.

"The guy must have a good job. He has to be well off. Of course he may have inherited a million."

"That's true, "Eunice said, "Martin, the rest of your group wanted to get pregnant within the month. I have to laugh. After all the honeymooning was over, six of the nine women present wanted to become pregnant."

Tony, Eunice's betrothed, remarked, "I heard what you said. The group counted on six pregnancies. That meant they would all give birth within a week of each other."

"Whoa, there are three couples who decided not to participate"

"Three out of nine is a good percentage. James and Loretta are still childless. They've been married a long time. He suggested they wanted to wait until he found a better job. Mary and Sheldon felt the same way about having children, but for a different reason. They bought a Motor Home and wanted to travel. I believe they have a trip planned for the East coast. I think she said Maine."

Eunice smiled, and butted in, "I had to beg off. Being single and having a baby is not socially correct in our group. I guess most of you had the same notion." She retreated, a step or two into the building's shadows.

"Who was it that planned the group pregnancies?"

"I believe Chela started the ball rolling. On the first show of hands, the group voted unanimously to approve the idea."

Eunice smiled again, "I don't have to ask what each of you will be doing after the park celebration here tonight. I'm sure you'll be making love. Would you say that was a good guess?"

Penny added a rejoinder, "It seems like the right thing to do. Before the vote took place, I hadn't really thought about it."

Tony added. "We haven't tied the knot yet, but I know I wouldn't trade a night like that for anything. We're not planning to have a child right away, but the excitement of the idea blows me a way."

Eunice butted in again, "Later, when the ladies began to show pregnancy, my first thought will be the special note the nurse at St. Mary's might offer to the families. I talked to her about pregnancy before Tony came. The gal is a winner. She's so thoughtful. She said, that for a large group she would assign all the babies to one area. That way, she could move the new born's into one corner of the nursery. After getting to know the mothers she felt she could do a better job with the infant babies closeted near each other. She also felt it would save time."

It was still that way the first week of April when the trouble started. The dawn opened up with several fleecy clouds spread across the sky. What had been a bright morning, full of sunshine the day before, was now overcast. The smell of moisture bore the presence of rain. It fit the day's ugly beginning.

Panic spread across the fourth floor of St. Mary's Hospital when the story leaked out. The night nurse, on the desk, said she found an envelope on the counter. Someone left a ransom note at the main desk suggesting the new babies had been placed in different beds. The letter stated that the correct replacement of the infants would be given once the ransom had been paid. When the story leaked out the women who were involved panicked. Several became hysterical.

Police officers began arriving at St. Mary's. Headquarters for the investigation was set up on the main floor. A call went out to Lieutenant Baldor. He was brought in to head the group. It was in the area he ordinarily patrolled. The Chief of Police at Headquarters hurriedly passed judgement on the appointment. Even though it was a high profile position he felt Baldor could handle it.

Baldor had gained a great deal of experience while working for the former Chief of Police, whom he even admitted, he missed. Assigning the task to the Lieutenant meant that no one would get their nose out of joint. In theory, the job belonged to Baldor.

Within the hour he gave the order, "I want that area partitioned off. I referring to the upper floor that contains the New Born Area of the hospital. I want to begin questioning those several hospital employees that had been on duty that night."

The manager of St. Mary's, was called Sarah.

She was the Mother Superior at both the hospitals.

Sarah quickly issued a statement, "We at St. Mary's wish to express our deep sorrow. The nurse who moved the newborns into one special area evidently made a mistake. It allowed some person, who is asking for a large ransom, to carry out the plan with ease. I want to advise you that our staff will cooperate in every way possible to bring this terrible crime to and end. Many of our employees after hearing about the nature of the crime, have come to us and offered their help in anyway possible. We will not change the position of any of the babies for now. That would be a disaster. If we find a solution, or we capture the criminal, it will go a long way toward easing the tension. Without that success there is hope that the new DNA procedure will provide evidence as to the exact placement of the babies, with their original parents. However the biological evaluation is so new that many of the mothers and fathers may look at the findings in disbelief. I'm hoping we will not have to rely on that technique for a final judgement."

The leader of security nodded his head. He went on to say that they would not rest until the culprit, or the culprits, could be brought to justice.

"I will not allow any of our people to take any extra pay for overtime while this situation is pending. We feel much of what happened can be attributed to some failure on our part."

She stood and came forward.

"You can be sure that we will find this person and give them their just reward. You can bet that reward will be a long time in jail. It's our best bet to wait until contact is made. By the way the chapel will be open all day, every day, until further notice. Those who wish to offer up a prayer on hospital property may do so without needing to inform our staff. If there is any need for medical help associated with the aftermath of this ugly state of events, St. Mary's will preform those primary services free of charge."

Mother Sarah stood and thanked the Security Manager for his testimonial. She had the sense that the group would not drag their feet. It made her feel as though the security staff might have the where-with-all to solve the problem. It would be a feather in her cap should that happen. Many board members had objected to her hiring the security company.

The previous experience of the small company was limited, and only one of the employees had a degree in surveillance technique. However, after two years of, on the job duty, many of her board members passed out accolades to the security group. They had operated without a slipup for 24 months. Now the board was on Mother Superior Sarah's side.

Unfortunately, it wasn't enough to prevent the calamity that befell the hospital. The censure now fell on the shoulders of the woman in charge. It was felt that her choice of board members had been lacking. Sure enough, the police had to place the blame on someone, and they chose Mother Sarah.

She took the abuse in a stride. It wasn't the first time she had been in the line of fire. Managing a large hospital with more than one thousand employed workers would never be an easy position from which to govern.

In the past, several mind-boggling interruptions had come to her door for disposition. In every case she was able to sidetrack the issue and gain the approval of the disheartened employees.

Sarah, the Mother Superior never minced words. After the eyeball to eyeball meetings no one felt they had been left out of the final decision. That kind of leadership was no longer prevalent in the modern day workplace. If it stood out anywhere, a hospital would likely be the place to watch a talent like that in action.

St. Mary's personnel was proud. They had chosen for them selves a genuine modern day politico. It was the tone of her voice that generally won the day. Nobilis oblige was a title that suited her makeup very well.

And so it was that fate laid this latest problem at the door of her office. It was a stinging reminder that leadership always bore the brunt of criticism, regardless of how remote that possibility might have become.

Somehow the staff knew that in just a few hours her judgement would fall on their ears. Much soul searching would pass between the workers. And many would try to place the blame somewhere else. Those futile attempts would soon be overcome by a weariness that quickly replaced any lackey's zeal.

It was then that saner thoughts brought further consideration to the fore. It was then that truth found a place, and it came as a surprise.

After two days of unrest and upheaval quiet became the reigning theme at the Carondelet Health Center.

Without too much effort, blame generally finds a place to hide. Today would be no exception.

Sarah, the Mother Superior knew just when to speak. She knew the old saying well, 'It's better, to be thought a fool, then to speak and remove all doubt.' She had never doubted the veracity of that statement, and for years it had served her well.

Sometimes in order to append the heft of that saying she willing would a tear and recite a time proven cliche. The cliche was as follows. 'And the end of all my journeys will be to arrive where I started, and know that place for the first time.'

When the flow of tears came she knew that everyone who witnessed the display would drop the discussion and relent. Now, letting her play winning game was as easy as falling off a log. Sister Sarah often used that avenue when desperation loomed. She had developed the technique to the point of utter perfection. Her closing statement always included some additional insurance, "When you want something you've never had before, you must do something you've never done before. When unleashed it acted like some ancient rapier about to become the tool of the winning side."

War always finds a willing antagonist. Nuns dressed in black and white habits proved to be the exception. Lacking horses and armor gave one the impression that any battle would find the other side victorious. Clearly that was not true. The novitiate held no blemishes on their record. A certain pride accompanied the valor that the nuns presented during each legal uprising. Some of the foes, they had defeated, were especially worthy of notice.

Three years ago the sisters had defeated the Attorney General of a neighboring state. Their efforts got them national recognition. On an occasion like that laurels got passed around, but an outstanding foe had not risen to the fore as of late.

Reputations die slowly. The Order of St. Mary's Carondelet was alive and well. The last victory had assured the young Nuns of a well-recognized reputation, which was much respected in the legal world. Very few lawyers wanted to tangle with the denizens of St. Mary's legal department. Their success record spoke for itself. One or two older lawyers were willing to take on the horde of young apprentices, but the majority of the new graduates wanted little to do with that part of the Hospital.

One of the young Harvard elite wrote an article in the New York Times stating, "it was grossly unfair to be pitted against forty-nine committed women of the faith." He added further that with that kind of time on his hands he too could excel.

One of St. Mary's chosen few wrote to the paper and demanded the lawyer withdraw the article and execute a public retraction.

She asked that her sister, Gwen, who was living in Denmark, be given credit for the convincing rejoinder.

In the newspaper business the combatants tend to know when the jig is up. The bureau chief threw in the towel the following morning. Accompanying the apology, the New York Times added the necessary vicissitudes. It turned out to be a well-placed jab in the tummy. After studying the effect of his denouncement the New York Times advised the reporter to do as St. Mary's asked. Squelching the article, via an apology was just a formality.

There was some rejoicing in the nunnery that afternoon. During the evening devotion, Sister Sarah handed out her always pleasant complements. The delightful lampoon got chuckles from the entire group.

The cub reporter wrote a followup which focused on a more personal side of the noteworthy article citing the fact that he had previously met Gwen in Denmark three years ago. Their second encounter happened when they met at a political rally a year later. His description off the tryst follows.

The meeting between the young lady and myself was perhaps at best, mere chance, but the impressions left behind had far reaching effects on both of us. We each sensed a magnetism generating between us, more like a biological glue that could not be easily explained.

It was to last for a significant period of time, and cemented the bonds of an incomprehensible lifelong friendship. We were both so alarmed that we kept it from the public's eye for a long time. In retrospect the reporter thought that Tracy and Hepburn might have held a similar attraction for each other.

Future clandestine meetings were effortless, "To peer into her innocent, hazel brown eyes, unflinching and attentive, and to imagine some yet to be learned treachery was traveling the country, searching for fair maidens to despoil ripped at my senses. However, this was the country she had chose to adopt, and Gwen was not one to be easily dissuaded."

In her quest for knowledge about the American heritage she read most every book that gave an account of the land across the ocean. So to, in her literary travels, Gwen acquired a working political knowledge of every major country in both hemispheres.

At one of our infrequent meetings, in the majesty of the moment, I sensed her naivete concerning the opposite sex, her willingness to react, unafraid and forthright. Struck by this obvious sincerity I knew she had not been sullied. A surge of mental relief flew by in my thoughts. Why I felt that way at the moment I'll never know. It was not a planned response, but it settled in my brain leaving me with a good feeling. Those thoughts bordered on what turned out to be the beginning of a silent prayer. So far the wretchedness which anchored so many lives, and with much heart rendering pity, had missed her. I still wonder why I felt such feelings, never having seen the young woman but twice before. The direction of that thought escaped me. Looking back, I now know I was smitten. Having fought against the idea for weeks after my first exposure, I knew we had a future together. However, difficult it might be.

The third time we bumped into each other I took a different physical position. I stood just a bit farther away from her than in our first and second exchange. It made it much easier to carry on a conversation at that distance. You see I was at a disadvantage. I had already been pillaged. I had been introduced to the seamier side of life long ago.

Not only did I see the shadow, but I was married.

It made me feel somewhat unworthy, talking with this gentle soul. So, I was the one who had to display a face totally devoid of carnal knowledge. I was the one who had to put on the air of honesty and purity: hard to do when one is aware of the pitfalls.

Morality comes much easier, when prior experiences refuse to take you into uncharted territory.

It was, as I remember, the summer of 1941. Ominous war clouds swept by on a daily basis blotting out all the charm of each, late autumn day. The warmth of summer played on both of us.

What confounded our conversation was a bizarre fact. We agreed that Americans could only envision a certain kind of death, by reading newspapers, or by listening to the radio. The killing of human beings, especially someone personally known escaped our thought processes. We, the citizens of this fair country were conditioned to believe we lived in the land of milk and honey.

For a long while our Government continued to operate in the haziness of Hedonism. For a longer time we foolish Americans followed the drum beat of illiteracy. The cry which went up from the pro-American standard keepers kept the questioning minority silent. Love it or leave was the folly of the few. Dissatisfied and militant, the accursed of the sixties died, or swung into the pecking order laid out for them to follow.

Years before, President Hoover had said, "A chicken in every pot and a car in every garage."

Laughter and a bit of added scorn graced that political statement long enough to lose him the office. In his place, there sat a man named Franklin Delano Roosevelt. Many of the voters thought the man was a Jew, and so voted against putting him in office. A great majority however thought he would take us out of the depression, and restore the once thriving country to its former greatness. Roosevelt tried, but twice he broke his wooden bat, without hitting a home run. All too soon, he became convinced that the way to prosperity lay in taking America to war. That was against his sworn promise. Some people say if he had not done so we, here, now, would be speaking German. Today, we know better.

One could espouse that Roosevelt's ego may have triggered our entry into World War II. That was undoubtedly true. Later I recall there were several attempts to warn the White House of an impending invasion by the Japanese, but dead ears led to Pearl Harbor and the killing began. The government quickly wrote off the deaths of thousands of soldiers who had fallen while serving their country. Washington ended by sending a pittance to the heirs. It all seems so shoddy. How much is a life worth? Can it be measured in terms of money?

I myself spent time in the military. That hitch I did took me to the South Pacific. It carved a hole in my efforts to find the arrhythmic American dream. It was not to be. A few metallic trinkets and the right to go to an institution of higher learning proved to be the residual of almost six years of 'I pledge allegiance to the flag.' While at a University, I was treated to a mostly liberal view point. At the time, it was the nature of the political beast.

Sometime after that, an elongated, introspective, but fanciful, dialogue occurred with Gwen. We exchanged our innermost thoughts. In a fit of bountiful energy, I found time to fall back to earth and bid the young lady good luck.

Luck had little to do with her success. Seriously, at that precise moment I felt as though I had been tongue tied. Quite obviously, she sensed my error in our solemn debate. Judgement time fell on both our shoulders.

She laughed coyly and in a light-hearted mood said, "Don't' let a few ill-chosen words order up your silence. We all slip up from time to time, don't we?"

It was then that she delivered a smile that I will carry in memory forever. It was not the faint smile which shown on the Mona Lisa. It was more robust, and not easily misconstrued. It was a jewel, a grand dessert, a memory picture I could not forget.

Then my mental digression came to a timely end.

I faced the rosy picture of the young lady about to launch herself into the next segment of a limited, but taunting time on earth. It would be noticed by everyone in the United States, and subsequently by more than half of the world.

Quite by chance, the young lady was introduced to another male reporter of some note. Intrigued by her approach to the top political problems, here and in the world, his interest became one of conviction.

At the time he noted, she had a complete and total grasp of the world and its impediments.

It was an astute appraisal. On balance she had shown an understanding far beyond what other young political emigres possessed.

I remember, she said that the conversation between the two wore on into the night. Thoroughly won over by her obviously truthful analysis the dean of newspaper reporters recommended her to the New York Times.

By the end of the week it was all over but the shouting. The young lady was hired on the spot. Within the week she had grabbed the spotlight on the op ed page. Her articles discussed the imminent dangers to America, which were present in the restlessness of young Moslems, alerted Government Intelligence. Through her inquiring comments they became aware. The impending Islamic danger had been circling their lackadaisical organization for a decade or two. From then on the media headlines quoted the female columnist on a daily basis. She had in just a short time become the spokesperson for all of America.

Her name was Gwen Fellowship. She was bright, outspoken, and quite eye catching. Yes, you could call her pretty. Hailing from a coastal city on the eastern side of the Atlantic ocean, she claimed to be Danish-American.

There was never a time when I did not follow her editorials. Some, I thought were fairly average, but in hind sight I now see how she had cleverly woven those reflections and facts into an amalgam of truth that held promise to all. Should her readers decipher and consolidate those editorial meanings the grip of understanding would forever be theirs. Her postulations were so insightful one could suspect a mole, in another political camp was feeding her tomorrow's headlines.

One never knows why a Supreme Being pours all the main ingredients of genius into one human being, knowing full well the dangers that are spawned from that over abundance. Due to physical and mental excesses that are a part of such a person, those in attendance stood transfixed in reverential awe.

At the end of our fourth meeting I suspected life would be

hard for a ripe plum such as Gwen. Her calling would not be a jolly existence. Her earthly assignment would be more to the depth of sorrow, more to the repugnant side of living. But through it all, she would find the zest for life that overrode the seamier part of her existence. The smile was always there, and the bell tones of her voice covered up whatever despair came into her spirited style of sprightliness.

Gwen was truly blessed, not only with a thumping good brain, but she carried the body of a Venus De Milo. And so it was, that our secret friendship began thanks in part to my continuous additions of circumlocution.

I could not fund my wealth of knowledge regarding her exploits. Egos can take a beating. Mine was ready for a chilling rejoinder. Soon after, Gwen became chief of the foreign bureau in Paris. I never saw her again. I never told my wife, and if she knew she never said a word. As for Gwen I made a conscious effort to rid my mind of any thoughts about her. Sure enough it worked.

* * *

On Saturday, Mother Superior gathered her staff together. It was her intention, after the breakfast prayer meeting, to offer her solemn praise. Her staff had stood behind her throughout the hazing by the newspapers and the rest of the media. The well orchestrated switch of the infants, and the subsequent ransom demand was pivotal. The early morning commentators asked for heads to roll. It was a silly coverup for suggesting that the Mother Superior be fired.

She in turn fired back, "First, I want to say this. If I'm sure that this room is no longer a safe place where I may speak and know that my voice will be frozen within these four walls, then by heaven I'll stop coming to St. Mary's. I will resign the very next day. I've been in many such debacles, but never one that comes out so soundly on the side of the accused. I thank you all for a job well done. It's pleasing to have a staff capable of genuine work ethics, and who care."

. She walked to a window and stared out.

Remembering a quote Sarah said, "In my earthly trials, God will offer his help, but not before I absolutely require it, otherwise I might begin believing I survived on my own. Several of you have been with St. Mary's a long time. You know I don't mince words. I always say what's on my mind, and I do it with as few words as possible."

Quite a few heads nodded in agreement. Some even clapped.

Sister Sarah continued her appraisal of her operational mode, "You know that I reward employees for good work, and you know that I honor my word. You also know, whatever positions open up that fit your abilities, it is likely, if you are interested, you can have a crack at the opening. That's been my absolute promise from the time I started running this hospital."

One of the head nurses spoke up; her station happened to be on the first floor. "What you say is true. I've availed myself of your way of passing out promotions. I handed in my application. Two days later, Sister Sarah called me into her office. She first said a prayer, then she handed me a set of the new duties that were involved in doing the task. Then we prayed together. Mother Superior shook my hand and I was out the door. I can tell you this, it's not easy going through the rig-a-ma-roll, but it is fair."

The nurse took a step backwards.

Adjusting her habit, she said, "Any job opportunity posted on the bulletin board can be investigated. There is that prospect. The petitioner could be chosen for the position. Just make sure you are up to the task. Sister Sarah dislikes shirkers. In fact, she'll make you pay the piper if you try to pull a fast one. She's been known to go hard on those that don't pull their weight."

The petitioner spoke, "I'm going to take a chance on being selected for the position. It is right down my alley. I've been doing this type of work for a long time, but unfortunately, it hasn't been in a professional setting."

"I don't believe that will make a difference. The Sister wants results. She'll be able to tell in a few questions just how capable you are. If you can cut it, I'm sure you will be rewarded with the new position. She'll let you know if you passed the test. She's quick to respond. I'm quite sure that someone, long ago, made her wait on the outcome of a position she had tested for. She didn't appreciate the time she spent hanging around on the hook of anticipation."

"Again, I want to thank the Mother Superior. She answered all my questions. I vote with the governing board that hired her. I know of no one who is better qualified."

Finished, the head nurse turned and walked out the door,

Investigative interviews went on the entire week. Police questioned the parents of the babies hoping to get additional evidence. They wanted to know who owned what babies. For the new mothers, the interrogation was insufferable. It was the worse thing that could have happened. It left the women afraid and unsure. Primarily, the fear stemmed from the outcome of the investigation.

Lieutenant Baldor, who was in charge, called for interrogations to begin the next morning. He was certain that someone might tell their story and it would lead to information that could help solve the case. The next morning six couples gathered in the office of St. Mary's Hospital. Why they were there was not known.

The Lieutenant had purposely kept them in the dark. He

stated, "Not being in the loop, they had no reason to call each other and compare notes."

Margaret and Martin had little to say. In the past, they had discussed births more than once. Eunice and Tony had not yet conceived a child. That closed the door on any information that they might have. Mary and Peter remained quite. George and Lorraine were ready to add their thoughts. Their testimony could be the most valuable to the police because it was true and had not been reviewed by the others.

Chela and Oscar just listened to the evidence.

Lorette and James had already admitted they were not going to participate, so along with Sharon and Sheldon that cut the witnesses to six.

Joyce and Raymond felt out of place. They had not been present at the hospital that day, so they felt it wasn't necessary to testify to any of the goings on.

Baldor spoke meaningfully to the two, "Your silence is not appreciated. I simply want an account of what you might have heard. It could go badly for you both. All I have to do is get a court order and you'll have to do as I ask. Do you want me to go through the motions, or will you do it the easy way?" Clarity forced them to reconsider.

A new mother got up from her chair and walked toward the Lieutenant. She spoke in a voice that demanded attention. "Mr. Baldor, please don't misunderstand me. We're not trying to be difficult. We simply don't know where our statement would fit in. We know what you are looking for, and I can tell you we have no evidence that would be of value to you. So I say to you, it would be better to approach others in the group that may have something to contribute."

The finish to her sentences ended the discussion for the day. The Lieutenant waved a hand and the meeting broke up for the day,

At the time, one disgruntled mother, later identified as Chela screamed in defiance. Losing her self control, she was placed in a ward with other women showing signs of being mentally disturbed. After her release her husband, Oscar, drove to the hospital and gently guided her to the car. He stayed awake the entire night tending to her needs. At about four that morning he managed to drift off in a troubled sleep.

CHAPTER II

That short nap produced a nightmare that lasted until he woke. The dream was so vivid, he thought he had really experienced it. That morning he brought breakfast to his mending partner. He insisted on telling her about the occasion of his dream.

He said to his wife, "You'll never believe this. After I fell asleep last night, I had this horrible nightmare. It was about a diamond mine in Africa. Somehow I got involved with another man, a seedy character by the name of Horace Bercan. We hailed a boat heading for the southern part of the African continent. We left the boat when it anchored on a channel that began near the tip of Africa. Horace, my new friend and I hurried to the first saloon to wet our whistles.

"Honey, let me tell the story from the beginning."

"That's fine with me."

"I'll call the dream, the Impus Diamond. Oh, by the way, in the dream I'm known as Millard Wren." His wife said, "That's very strange. Why, in your dream, would a different name be used?"

"I've always been called by the name I'm using now. Shucks, I want to, and I will recite this story just as I remember it."

Millard Wren and Horace Bercan, two nondescript, itinerant dock workers met during a rainy night at a local beer parlor just outside of town. It was in the southern part of Africa near the coast. Both men needed work. Hearing that the BeMeers Co. Ltd., owners of several diamond mines, needed more workers, both men planned to apply for openings in the non-union positions. After filling out the questionnaire regarding hiring practices BeMeers hem each a job.

. Thievery was their goal. Stealing a diamond from their employer would satisfy their greed, so they felt they had crossed the first hurdle.

When he was sixteen, Millard Wren left the State of Indiana; drunken parents forced him out of their home. Miles of highway and long, dreary days got him to the east coast. When the army threatened to draft men of his age, he took passage on a tramp steamer. Shipboard, searching for new adventure, he headed for the African Continent.

Horace Bercan, another American, born in England, also dreamed of striking out on his own. His parents had the itch to be more than shopkeepers, so they sold their shoe store in the south of England and migrated to America. Horace wanted no part of that dull existence. His parents made the mistake of leaving a large sum of cash loose in the house. Finding the money in an upstairs bedroom drawer, he quickly packed a suitcase.

Horace had frugal parents. Appalled when they found that the money was missing, along with their son, they contacted the police.

Horace knew that staying in America was the last thing he should do, so he booked passage on a tramp steamer. Traveling to the continent of Africa, he too, decided to seek employment.

BeMeers Mines Ltd. was actively expanding their holdings. In the employment line, Horace began discussing a plan with Millard

Wren, the man in line directly behind him. Both men carried an overriding wish…to make it big in Africa: somehow, steal a diamond, of good size, and escape taking passage on the first boat to America. It was an easy decision for them to make. Later that night, Millard and Horace further cemented their friendship by pooling resources. Going back to the same beer parlor, they drank a few more warm beers. After the third one, they shook hands and formed an alliance which carried them to an unusual end.

Relatively uneducated, both men displayed a certain coarseness in their manners and in their conversation. Acting arrogantly in public mattered little to them: Blunt chatter and ingrained insolence were as natural as defecating. Yet, each displayed qualities, which had matured in that rough, tough existence. It became a vital part of their plans. To them, it meant carrying through on their scheme to get rich. Intellectually, they had all the baggage they needed to succeed: A crude collection of guile and perseverance, as well as a crafty approach to any endeavor that spelled reward. Pooling resources allowed Wren and Bercan to reach the Sagen mine just weeks before BeMeers announced the discovery of the largest gem ever found. The BeMeers called it the Impus Diamond. At the time, neither man bothered trying to steal the gem. They felt its size would make it difficult to turn into hard cash. However, fate intervened and galvanized their actions. Destiny placed them on the doorstep of untold wealth, and as it turned out, their demise.

CHAPTER III

Faulty supervision and timing allowed the Impus Diamond to go unattended overnight, just two days after its discovery. It was then that a trusted worker in the wash area removed the gem. In total darkness, he carried the Impus Diamond to the Bolango, an abandoned gold mine, also owned by BeMeers. Burying the stone, he made a rough drawing for future reference. Foresight and its partner, Lady Luck, handed the original map to Millard and Bercan. The drawing pointed to the diamond's location. It was now in their hands to succeed. Unfortunately, others also showed an interest, others who were more resourceful, others who had more cunning. Yes, there were others, who played the game for keeps.

I was privy to this extraordinary tale just after my twenty first birthday. It was told to me, in a haphazard fashion, over a span of several weeks, and represented an eye-socking, brain-rattling slice of life. I tell it as it came to me through the twisted minds and gut feelings of the diverse characters involved. I make little pretense of being a finished, acclaimed story teller; I'm only a chronicler. At times, while immersed in the story, I found myself to be confounded, and always somewhat naive: Considering the circumstances, it left me shocked, doubting, and unsure of the promised future. I was un able to vouch for the truth of the lurid events that took place in this short recounting, but I'm quite certain that by reading these few pages they will treat your senses to a delightful, mind-boggling, literary romp. The word-picture is yours to enjoy. So, its time to begin this fascinating tale of adventure and intrigue.

* * *

Cataracts portend deep drops in the passage of rushing water. Ahead, a deafening roar signaled a waterfall. From shear-sided cliffs, Kintu Falls plunged two hundred feet to a basin-shaped gorge. Jagged boulders, worn smooth by the turbulent water, lined both shores. Dense spray, from the flume, rose above the unending rocks, creating a lavish fog. Pummeled by the white water, Wren's dingy began taking on water. For the first time, Millard experienced a knot of fear in his stomach. Wiping a sleeve across his brow, he studied the surging current. Petrified, he grabbed the gunnels of the dingy and addressed his plight.

Yelling toward the gorge, he swore repeatedly, "Asshole. You've lost Bercan. He has the map, and you let it get away. You're a real dummy. The colossal mistakes, you and your partner make on this venture are legend. Does Irish heritage have to make you act like an idiot?"

CHAPTER IV

Millard, was not a handsome man. A chiseled nose, and large, luminous, brown eyes set off high, pale, cheek bones. Milk-white skin covered the rest of his small, pockmarked features, making for an interesting face. Occasionally, a lock of auburn hair drifted by his forehead. At times he limped. This made him look like an elf. A violent encounter with the law, left his right-leg a bit shorter. Two bullets had angered the flesh. The bone, broken in three places, had knitted poorly. Ashamed of his noticeable hobble, Millard had learned to walk in a hip-pity-hop fashion.

"There it is," he stammered. The rising mist focused his anxiety even further.

"In a few hundred yards, this boat is going over Kintu Falls. I'm going to have one heck of a time staying alive."

Tons of angry water catapulted him into the tumbling, white cascade. The projection was well past the initial tumult. Fortune and the boat's speed had driven him beyond the froth into open air: Time enough to assess his quandary. Glancing down, Wren knew that plunging that distance would be fatal.

"Think Wren," he yelled, "think! You've only got seconds."

Crouching low in the dinghy, leg muscles coiled, Millard

readied himself. Just before the wooden craft met solid water, he pushed up with his feet, off the bottom of the boat. That effort in slowing his fall became a manageable velocity: an action that gained him a new lease on life.

Cleared of the dinghy, gravity drove him deep into the boiling cataract: a downward plunge that carried him well below the water's surface. Propelling himself upward, he reached the surface. He gulped a lung full of air and smiled broadly.

He kept repeating, "Miracle, it's a miracle. My chances of living were very poor. Luckily, Irish Cats always land on their feet."

Looking back at the deluge, he raised an index finger and crawled onto the white sandy beach. Torpidly, he recalled the last hour.

"Who would believe me? Going over Kintu Falls should have ended my life. At least now, Shields is no threat. If he saw me go over, perhaps for him, my trail ends. It would help to know if I have some breathing room."

Millard Wren gave the territory a quick eye.

"It looks safe," he mused, "no crocodiles." Stretching out full-length on the sand, a troubled nap edged over him. It would be an hour before he knew Shields had viewed the total scene—saw him bob to the surface and make for shore. From a distance, Shields smiled. He still had a warm trail.

Short, squat, mean, and forever slovenly, Shields in many ways mimicked the devil. In his younger days, the schoolyard provided the backdrop for his hellish behavior. Smokey black eyes and an olive skin that always showed a dirty tinge gave him an ugly appearance.

Cruelty to others because it gave him a sense of power, Shields always found a way to mistreat people. He had kicked a young boy, Darcy Marks, in the testicles three weeks into the school term. Darcy never returned to school. After that incident, anyone going to classes that Shields' attended was concerned. A rabid, constant fear lived in each of the students. That gave Shields what he wanted, unbridled control.

Darcy's father never complained. Thoughts of what might have happened had he acted, immobilized him. One week later arson provided a measure of proof. A blazing fire at the Marks' home gave promise of additional misery. It was the crowning obstacle to any recounting of a diabolical prank. By the weekend, it had turned into a complete Shields' victory.

For three years, after dropping out of school, Shields drifted from job to job. In the middle of the fourth year he signed on as a deck hand aboard an ocean going vessel named the Moria Gay. Forced to work eleven hour shifts as a laborer angered him. So he jumped the ship at Cape Agul-has, a South African port of call. The captain of the ship never reported the incident. Factually, he was glad to be rid of the trouble maker.

Now Shields' ugly talent would make a difference. Here, in this part of the world, might would often make right. In the next eight years, using abhorrence and his greed, together, he carved out an evil empire.

Hirelings, paid to report any signs that might lead to ill-gotten profit, spearheaded his organization.

Recently, the story of a missing diamond perked his senses. Shields repeated a general theme to his henchmen.

"That piece of carbon will change my lifestyle and yours. My eight-year search for enough money is over. Success means a chance to return to the States."

Perseverance paid off. An informer relayed the right bit of gossip, and the trail got warm.

The informant reported, "There were two men who buried

the body of the thief. They must have found something. Why else would they quit their jobs?"

"Good work," Shields replied, "they must have money to live on. You can bet there's hidden cash somewhere close by. Watch them both. I think they are the keys to a good chunk of wealth. We could be looking for the Impus Diamond."

During the daylight hours, Shields' group stalked both Millard and Bercan. Fear of retaliation by Shields kept them vigilant. As the night shift reported for duty, the boss, Shields, doubled the number of men he had on patrol. He did not intend to allow their escape.

The man's wife Chela, rolled over in the bed and said, "This sounds like it may take a few minutes. I have to visit the bathroom to pee. Can you hold up on the story until I get back?"

"Sure. No problem. I'm positive. The story will only last about ten minutes, no more."

Martin's wife returned and he began again.

Horace Bercan, who had become Wren's unwilling partner, gave life to the cliche, "The Convict's Mind." Every inch a criminal, Horace needed incessant watching. Even when he lived at home he needed supervision. His loathing of the life he was living brought him to a plan. He had to get away.

His father often carried large sums of cash in his wallet. It was easy Pickens. The money stolen from his parents got him to the coast of southern Africa. Hearing Bercan's story, Wren verbally reprimanded his associate's, pecuniary approach.

"Filling your pockets, in whatever way possible, means you're a low life, but if it answers your needs, I don't care. Should I trust you? Huh, even though I'm your partner, but I'm keeping my eyes open. Pulling that shit on me won't work."

Oily skinned, unshaven, and always wearing a sly smile augured for the mistrust Wren accorded his partner. Oddly, both held a healthy respect for each other.

Commitment came after a night of drinking beer in Flex's tavern. Both men became drunk. Not flinching, after the outburst Wren had just reeled off, Bercan smiled, and spoke in a patronizing tone.

"Ah, that's not the way I see it at all. You're my partner. I'm giving you my word. Trust me. Wait till I screw up before you start yelling. The guy you should watch is that ugly little fellow who was setting in the back room away from the bar. Wasn't his name Shields?"

Shields often thought about the notches on his gun-butt, one for each life he had taken. Disposing of fifteen people made him smile. It tickled him, snuffing out human life. He never felt remorse. Laughing while the blood flowed, he got a kick out of watching his quarry squirm. Because of his ugly actions the men working for him had little respect, but they did fear him.

Taking a pull on the bottle of rye whiskey, Shields yelled, "Minus a foot, minus a hand, or skewered in the belly with a knife, I enjoy watching their pumps slowly quit."

Ending each life with some type of mutilation, Shields reveled in the gore. "I do have space for two more notches on my gun," he acknowledged. "It's time to add a notch or two to the butt of my gun. I've got just the two idiots that fit the bill." Ending this perception, he returned his thoughts to the Impus Diamond.

Suspecting that possibly the diamond lay hidden at the Bolango, twenty miles south of the Sagen mine, Shields had added three additional men to cover the perimeter. Posting the men on the north and east corners of the town, he said, "Keep those two under surveillance. Those are the orders. The prize is a drawing or a map of where the diamond might be." Shields let a smile break out, again, "The drawing ought to show the abandoned Bolango. It's the nearest, likely spot. Rumors had placed the buried Impus Diamond five hundred feet from the entrance: three feet west of the last curve and marked by an Indian laborer's femur bone." Still guessing, Shields began piecing together the theft and the burial.

The flat empty space south of the wash area had been left unprotected for over a year. Jackals and hyenas scoured the land nightly for food. Their success kept workers from venturing in that direction. One worker at the mine had a different thought. It was the true path to freedom.

From the wash area north of the Sagen Mine, the itinerant worker made off with the uncut stone. Leaving the cleaning acreage, he traveled twenty miles south to the Bolango. Crossing the BeMeers' border unobserved was a bit of luck. On the way back, search lights picked up his movements. After yelling 'Halt' a burst of machine gun fire ripped through his body. Guards reported the incident, but associating the Impus Diamond, with the man's death appeared remote. He was traveling north back to the camp, not south.

BeMeers officials let the episode drop. Headed the wrong way, the intruder escaped consideration as a suspect.

Ordered to dispose of the corpse the following day, Wren and Bercan left the next morning to bury the body. Finding an open pit a mile from camp, they dumped the carcass and topped it off with a few shovels of dirt. Before burial, however, they checked the man's pockets and found a notebook-sized sheet of paper. Not understanding the scribbles at first, they later realized it was a detailed drawing of an abandoned mine.

Bercan stuffed the diagram in his oilskin pouch and began yodeling, "In my hand is the path to wealth and to going home." Kissing the pouch, he said, "Oh baby, I hope this leads to the Impus. You know what that would mean?"

Millard turned to his partner and grinned. Having found the map, the change in their attitudes forced a new set of rumors to abound.

BeMeers' authorities, not wanting to publicize the loss of the diamond, never asked the men about those rumors, and of course the two men never volunteered.

"We're the only ones who know for sure where the Impus is hidden," Bercan remarked, jumping up and down. "Do you hear what I'm saying?" Millard Wren looked at him stiffly.

"Listen, keep your mouth shut, lay low, be casual. Let's choose the right time to hunt for the stone."

Bercan began squealing, "The whole camp thinks we have the answer. Like hawks, they're watching every move we make."

"Horace, knock it off. Let them think what they want. We can wait. We've got enough cash to manage. By waiting we'll have a better chance. Loitering around town the next two weeks will sidetrack everyone. Agreed?"

Not knowing the location of the gem, Shields needed directions. Showing impatience, he walked back to his camp.

On a hunch, he told his men, "If my suspicions are correct, the grave diggers will lead us to the gem. Keeping your eyes on them is important. Remember that I'm spending a ton of money on this fishing expedition. Paying for the guns, the ropes, and the other gear is expensive. I don't like getting the short end of the stick." A long swig of coffee forced him to stop talking.

"No one is going to cheat me out of that rock. I've waited a long time for this chance. Hell...BeMeers claims the diamond is flawless, a pure light blue stone. Delivered to the right place, it will easily bring ten or twelve million dollars." He turned and faced his men. "Let's be ready. You there, stop bobbing back and forth, yeah, you on the end. Don't get antsy. We'll be under way soon."

BeMeers, the owners of the gem, unexpectedly acknowledged

the theft. They posted the information on the company bulletin board along with a retrieval notice. The retrieval notice gave directions on how to report to BeMeers and how to take advantage of the company's offer for safe passage away from the area. BeMeers had a reputation for honesty in their dealings. Most of the workers felt they could trust the CEO.

Stephen Barco, the president of BeMeers, gave the following statement, "Anyone finding the gem may return it to the office, no questions asked. We expect to reward the individual. BeMeers offered a payment of twenty thousand pounds. The reward will be settled the same day. Besides the reward, we will provide safe passage out of Africa."

That offer was made with guarded reservation. Indeed, it was the last announcement the company wanted to make. That disclosure created an open season for finding the stone.

Mr. Shields was sitting in the bar drinking some rye whiskey he heard about the offer.

He laughed insidiously, "What fool would take advantage of that paltry reward. I'll tell you this, not me?" Most of the other members of the group felt the same way.

Bercan, pulling away from the gathering, nudged his partner, "Hey Millard, I think Barco's crazy. Who'd leave twelve million behind? Freedom and twenty thousand English pounds will get no takers."

Wren, thoughtfully agreed, "You're right. It would be idiotic to turn down a fortune in exchange for peanuts. What's that dumb saying? A bird in the hand is worth two in the bush. For once, we agree on something."

Growling, Bercan honed in on a new thought.

"Wait a minute, why be pigs. We should go for the sure bet. Take the company's offer and a safe trip out of here. What good is it if we never get a chance to spend the cash?"

Wren, let out a low chuckle. Deep down, he was thinking the same way.

"What a good feeling that would be" he said. "Escorted out of Africa, courtesy of the sheltering arms of BeMeers is not all bad. In your dreams there's no chance of that happening."

"Why say that? Didn't the Company promise safe passage to those who asked for special consideration?"

"Sure, but that doesn't mean that they will honor their words. You know how big companies get ahead, they lie, cheat and steal. Why would they change just now for us? It's all boloney sauce. If you buy that, you're more stupid than I gave you credit for."

"Look. Things change. People and the companies they run find that past practices have no place in the modern world. The newly educated, graduates know that a labor force that's happy is a plus. The old fashioned, 'treat the employees rough' doesn't cut it anymore. Strikes are too expensive, and when the strike is over very few of the employees forget. The hurt feelings hang around for years. Sometimes they influence what happens during the next labor negotiations. New management understands that company attitude goes a long way in settling the disputes. Bargaining between the groups in a fair but practical way assures a good outcome and heals previous wounds."

"Your point is well taken. I've been for that type of action all my adult life."

The talk slowed to silence, and the two joined in the march to the mess hall.

By now, the media considered the story their biggest news item in years. Reporters flocked there, trying for a firsthand account. However, each inquiry further distorted the facts. Several press releases suggested that Millard Wren and another man, Horace Bercan, had stolen the raw gem from the Sagen Mine. Clamoring for more information, reporters continued to print any half-truths they managed to find. When Wren read the stories, he swore.

"The bastard wants to get us hung. You know, every hungry con man, in the area, is watching."

His partner nodded.

"We should go after the diamond now. Find it, and get the hell out of here."

Nettled, Wren kept denying his partner, "Cripes, that's what they want. Do you think I'm nutty? That would be a dead-give-away. Why don't you use your noodle? You know, that it's easy to be stupid."

"Don't get on my ass. You've pulled a couple of boners yourself. I've had the dubious honor of seeing two of them. So knock-it-off, will you."

Millard framed an answer, "Piss on you. Remember. The brains in this outfit belong to me."

"Ah, that's bullshit," Bercan replied. They looked at each other, grinned, and started to laugh.

Bercan continued wheedling, "Let's find the stone now. We can claim the reward and beat it out of here. We have the map; that's one leg up. What do you say?"

A thought settled over Wren...

"Okay, let's go for it. Hang onto the map. Without it, we don't have a prayer." Bercan pointed to his breast pocket.

"Don't worry. I've got it right here, and it's safe."

That same night they packed their gear. An interested person noted their movements. The lookout for Shields hurried back to the bar where the head man was having a nightcap.

He approached Shields and blurted out his observation, "I think they're getting ready to leave."

"What do you mean," Shields asked?

"They're packing their gear, and they already paid off their room rent."

Shields signaled his men. In less than half an hour they shouldered their equipment, and headed south. Shields figured the two thieves would head south toward the Kintu River. He made the right guess.

Already on the trail, Wren and Bercan felt the sting of Shields' plan. They had not realized that their pursuer had placed a tracker near their rooms.

After an hour of following the map, Bercan turned to his partner, "If, we can stay hidden for a couple days of the journey, our trail will be cold."

Millard chuckled, again, "That's a good approach. I think we can do that."

The glint of a rifle barrel on the third day told them a different story. Staying out of sight was not that easy. Speed became important. Laboriously hacking a trail through the undergrowth took its toll. Raw blisters festered, and swelled. Puffy fingers made it onerous to handle the heavy machetes.

Breath came in short pants. The effort forced them to take a new tack, one that would grow into a monestrous mistake.

"I can't go on without a rest. Damn, can't you see I'm bushed."

"Look. You're not alone. My heart feels like it wants to quit, but we've got to keep going. Horace, it's only another mile or so. We have the edge, so let's keep that cushion."

Exhausted, they slowly slashed their way toward their trump card, a dinghy hidden on the shore of the Kintu. Some weeks before, Wren, following the river, had discovered the old dingy.

Bellowing against the jungle din, he quipped, "We'll leave Shields and his trackers behind when we find the dinghy. Once we lose them, we won't feel the pressure. Hell, they won't know where we're going."

Bercan saluted, "Millard, your idea of traveling the river is a winner. Damn...I'm glad we have the boat. We can use the rest."

"I told you. I've got the brains in the outfit"

Bercan pointed a finger into the air, "Don't break your arm patting yourself on the back."

Both men knew the river flowed south…and that using the river would be an advantage. That's when Wren started happed-hopping along the shore.

"What's the matter? Why are you hurrying?" Bercan asked. "Anyone might think you've got a bug in your pants."

Millard Wren grunted, and waved his arm toward a point on the hill behind them. Bercan caught the shining glint of steel among the high boulders. Shields and his six lieutenants were only a few hours behind.

"Damn they've seen us. Listen, our plan will only work if we use common sense. We need to keep going. We can't drop our guard for a minute."

"Yeah, I know. Shields, is not easy to fool, Bercan replied, but it surprises me that he's that close."

Doubling their efforts, Wren took the lead.

Angling further south he began cutting another path with his knife. Palm trees, short green bushes, water soaked ground and insects continued to hamper their progress. When Wren tired, Bercan moved ahead and began slicing through the mat of green growth. For an hour he chopped at the bramble. Both men's hands were bleeding profusely. Then, Horace threw his knife on the ground. Weary, close to exhaustion, he stopped.

"I know they're right behind us, but I'm so tired I don't care. I need some rest."

"We'll take a short break, but no more."

* * *

Shields, remembering the handsome reward, yelled from a small knoll, "Keep those two idiots in sight. If we lose their trail, we could lose the diamond. Son-of-a-bitch, I've come too far to miss the payoff."

A guide spoke up, "You know, they're heading due south. I wonder how that's going to help them. They've got to go around the Falls. Maybe they intend to use ropes to lower themselves to the canyon floor."

For a moment, the group was silent.

Shields, sensing he had made a mistake, gave an order, "You two, go back to base camp. It's only a couple of miles. Follow the path we made, and bring those coils of rope. If they use ropes to go down the cliff, we will too. Hurry! Do you hear me? Hurry!"

Wren and Bercan realized one fact. They had time on their side. After resting, they traveled steadily south. Hearing the river's rush ahead, Wren stopped and yelled. "We must be getting close. The Kintu can't be more than a mile from here."

Bercan nodded, "I hear it. It's making sweet music to my ears."

Increasing their gait, the river's throaty roar exploded over the next rise. Exhaling slowly, Wren's face lit up, signaling freedom.

Heading for a clump of palm-fringe, he hollered, "Listen, to that music. It's our ticket out. Didn't I tell you I had covered all the bases?" Feeling peeved and unsure, Horace looked back at Millard.

"Baloney, I believe we should stay and ambush the bastard. We'll never be safe until that son-of-a-bitch quits breathing. You know he won't give up. Let's stop on high ground and go for a showdown, right now."

Above the noise, Wren shouted, "You're crazy, he has six men with him. Seven against two, I don't like the odds. Sure he hangs on like a pit-bull, but the distance between us will cool him down. We can always stand and fight. I'm betting we can find a better place than this to face him."

"You're chicken," Bercan replied. "Surprise is our big edge.

He'd never believe we'd attack against those odds. That's why I say, clobber him now. We could nail two or three of his goons before they knew what hit them."

"Shut up," Wren said, "you make me tired with your fanciful daydreams. Your silly ideas haven't got a prayer. We've come this far, hacked through half a jungle, and are way ahead of Shields. We have the prize in our pocket. Why should we throw the diamond away just to prove how brave we are? Use your common sense. Our chances of surprising Shields aren't worth a tinker's dam."

"Well, at least you know how I feel," Bercan said, kicking at a green branch hanging low to the ground. He didn't notice a horde of red ants swarm onto his leather boot. The first sting directed his attention, and a tirade of oaths followed. Bercan began stomping his feet on the ground.

While attempting to dislodge them, he yelled, "Fire ants! They sting!" Violently beating at the swarm of crawling insects with his glove, he scraped at them. A few he killed, others fell to the ground. With his fingers he picked off the rest.

"Did you get them all?" Millard asked. "Those pesky beasts can carve a hole in your leg in minutes."

"Yeah, I think so," Bercan answered. "Geez, doesn't anything go right?"

"Well, if you're ready to travel? Let's move out. I know we can make our next camp close to the Bolango mine." He paused and then made a motion to get up.

"Whatever you say, but let's get away from those fire ants. They give me the Willies."

The thought started Bercan shivering.

Millard interjected, "That episode is over. Forget it. Think about home and America. Thinking about spending the money is on my mind. I'd like to settle down, buy a car, maybe a house."

Coming to a small glen in the jungle, Bercan began complaining. "Wren, I'm bushed; I need to rest. Can we stop? We really can't afford it, but chopping through that undergrowth is hard work. We can work at it for ten minutes, but that's all. I need a rest."

"Okay, ten minutes, but no more."

The rest turned into a prolonged sleep. Steaming hot, the African jungle woke Bercan at high noon. He looked at his watch and yelled, "Millard, Millard! We screwed up!"

"Now what's the matter?" Then, Wren looked at the time. "For Cramps sake, we've over slept. How long have you had your eyes open?"

"I guess about two minutes," Bercan replied.

"We blew our lead. Now, they're right behind us. Of all the dumb tricks we've pulled, this is the worse. I'm sure Shields kept marching. He'd be a fool if he didn't. Look. Isn't that the gang that's after us?"

Shields also them, and started yelling, "I've got them in my sights. The idiots made camp, and now we're looking down their throats."

Gathering their packs, Wren and Bercan's forced march worked south to the river's shore. The shorter man began protesting.

"Man. The heat is unbearable. How hot is it? The temperature must be more than a hundred degrees. Wren, I need a drink."

"Here's the canteen," Millard said, "go easy, it's all we have."

"Yeah, we should have brought more." Swallowing the warm water, Bercan handed back the canteen. "Say, what's that noise. It's really thunderous."

"That's the Kintu's roar. It's louder, so we're close. Ten minutes and we'll be there."

Reaching the river, they searched for the dilapidated dinghy, covered with palm leaves. To the right and barely visible the boat lay semi-hidden in jungle green growth. Millard Wren moved forward and stripped away the emerald camouflage. With a throaty rasp, he righted the boat. Both he and Bercan shoved the small craft into the water. Managing to balance the small boat, they boarded.

"Where are the oars?" Millard asked. "You forgot them? Horace, can't you do anything without screwing up?"

"Okay, so why get into an uproar," Bercan replied. "Let's take the boat back to shore."

Millard pointed toward the shore, "The oars are near the tree limb to the left of the palm leaves."

Beaching the boat about a hundred yards downstream, Bercan jumped out. Just as he found the paddles, the sound of a gun shot echoed off the canyon walls. A spent slug jammed its way into Bercan's fleshy leg. Grabbing both oars in his arms, he hobbled back to the boat.

"Get out of here," he screamed, pointing at his bleeding leg.

"The son-of A bitch just shot me." Scrambling back aboard, Bercan tossed the oars to his partner. Millard quickly attached the metal oars to the gunnels. Pointing the craft downstream, he pulled at the oars with all his remaining strength. The current helped. It dragged the boat to the center of the river where a bend in the waterway increased their feeling of 'getting out of sight.' Parking the oars, Wren started tending to Bercan.

"You're damn lucky," he announced. "It just grazed your leg."

"God, it really hurts."

"Ah, shut up. What the hell would you do if you had a bullet in your chest or your head?"

"Don't lay that crap on me," Bercan yelled. "I've never had a hole in me before. It's smarting and really burns."

Millard whistled, "Maybe it's worth it. We're getting away

from Shields. That should count for something. I think we're damn lucky. When you give that bloodhound the slip you know your fortune has changed."

"Is that roar, the rapids, or a waterfall?" Bercan asked. "I don't know," Wren said. "We'll have to wait and see." After he bound Bercan's leg, Millard watched his partner's face turn to a questioning look.

"It has to be a waterfall, look at the rising mist," Wren replied, "but it can't be very high." Bercan looked at the mist-shrouded, canyon walls.

"I'm not going over that drop-off. I'll take my chances on shore." In a panic, he didn't give Wren an opportunity to suggest a counter plan. Bercan dove over the side of the dinghy. He started swimming toward the shore.

"Your idiot, come back," Wren shouted, "this is 'choc' country. Crocodiles are all along the shore!" A prayer crossed Wren's lips. "Please let Bercan make it to shore. He's got the map. Without it, I don't have anyway of finding the diamond. This whole effort would be for nothing if the map gets lost. Now, I'd better tend to the problem of going over the falls."

Cataracts portend deep drops in the passage of rushing water. Ahead, a deafening roar signaled a waterfall. From shear-sided cliffs, Kintu Falls plunged two hundred feet to a basin-shaped gorge. Jagged boulders, worn smooth by the turbulent water, lined both shores. Dense spray from the flume rose above the slippery rocks, creating a profuse fog. Pummeled by the white rapids, Wren's dingy began taking water. For the first time, Millard Wren experienced a knot of fear in his stomach. Wiping a sleeve across his brow, he studied the surging current. Petrified, he grabbed the gunnels of the dingy and addressed his plight.

Yelling into the gorge, he swore repeatedly, "You're a damnable dimwit. You've lost Bercan. You knew he had the map, and you let it get away. That was not very smart, I guess we both trashed the success of this venture.

"I thought history recorded that the Irish were smart, but here I stand. I'm acting as if I'm the class idiot, and it not what I should be doing."

Millard, was not a handsome man. A chiseled nose, and large, luminous, brown eyes set off high, pale, cheek bones. Milk-white skin covered the rest of his small, pockmarked features, making for an interesting face. Occasionally, a lock of auburn hair drifted by his forehead. At times he limped. This made him appear elfish. A violent encounter with the law, left his right-leg a bit shorter. Two bullets had angered the flesh. The bone, broken in three places, had healed poorly. Ashamed of his noticeable hobble, Millard had learned to walk in a hip-pity-hop fashion.

"There it is," he stammered. The rising mist focused his anxiety even further.

"In a few hundred feet, this boat is going over Kintu Falls. I'm wagering I'll have one heck of a time staying alive."

Diving into the tumbling, white cascade, tons of angry water catapulted him past the initial tumult. Fortune and the boat's speed drove him beyond the froth into open air: Time enough to assess his quandary. Glancing down, Wren knew that plunging that distance would be fatal.

"Hey, you're an idiot," he yelled, "think! You've only got seconds." Crouching low in the dinghy, leg muscles coiled, Millard readied himself. Just before the wooden craft met solid water, he pushed up with his feet as hard as he could, off the bottom of the boat. That effort, in slowing his fall, became a manageable velocity: An action that gained him an additional lease on life.

Clear of the dinghy, gravity drove him deep into the boiling cataract: A downward plunge that carried him well below the water's surface. Propelling himself upward to the surface, Wren gulped air and smiled broadly.

He kept repeating, "Miracle, it's a miracle. My chances of living were... Luckily. Irish Cats do land on their feet."

Looking back at the deluge, he raised an index finger and crawled onto the white sandy beach. Torpidly, he recalled the last few minutes. It began with Bercan swimming for the shore.

His partner, Bercan, began making toward the far, western shore of the river. Bercan could hear Wren yelling something, but the roar of the falls drowned out the ominous word, crocodile. Horace had swum too within a hundred feet of land when he saw a large, grey-green form scrambling toward the river. Boiling water followed the splash. The reptile had spotted a meal in its favorite hunting area. Huge in size, the crocodile smoothly parted the dark green liquid, driving its long armored tail toward the frenzied swimmer. Moments later, its large, golden eyes appeared near the surface.

"Now I know why Wren kept yelling." Watching the crocodile glide toward him, he yelled, "It's over the falls now, or let that reptile rip me to shreds." Pulling at the water with cupped hands, he steadily maintained his distance. Sensing danger, the reptile lunged at its prey. Bercan thrashed the water, trying to reach the mouth of the falls. His left leg jerked painfully as the reptile clamped down with his teeth.

"Get away, get away," Bercan screamed. The beast twisted its body in a rolling motion. That made the muddy, dark water turned to froth, and Horace Bercan's leg came loose at the knee. The crocodile got a small meal; Kintu Falls got the balance of the carcass.

Washing up on shore, about a mile downstream from Millard, Bercan remains had already begun to decompose.

A scant thirty minutes had passed since Bercan dove over the side of the dinghy.

Shields marched on. He knew how to track his quarry closing in behind Wren again. From his vantage point, the tracker, had viewed the entire episode. He smiled again.

Rising to its zenith, the sun's rays scorched the ground. For a few seconds, Wren stirred uneasily on the shore, then he rolled to his right. Something prodded him to look back at the plunging water. His conscious mind focused. He sat bolt upright, staring at the falls. For an instant it looked like an object had hurtled over the edge, losing itself in the spray.

"Wasn't that Bercan? Why did he go over the falls now? I must be dreaming." Millard blinked, and rubbed the moisture from his eyes.

"Christ, if that's Horace, he's dead meat. I'd better move down to the edge of the river. He should surface somewhere upstream from here. If he's alive, we can continue. Shit, if he's dead... I still need that map."

Millard Wren began cutting a path alongside the river. Stroke after stroke, his machete sliced down and through the thick, green foliage. By noon, he was a few hundred feet from Bercan's bloated form.

Intense heat had already started to wrestle the meat from Bercan's body. Insects of every description climbed into and out of the rotting torso. The air, alive with the stench, carried his presence to every living animal. Shields noticed also.

Though farther away, one of his guards had made a foray quite close to the area. After finishing the new trail the odor became stronger. In a matter of minutes he stood over the man's lifeless form. Bercan's smell had alerted him. Returning to camp he reported to Shields. Hearing the scout's report, the head man moved his men swiftly down to the river's edge.

Excitement rode through the camp. Every man had his own dream tied to the chase.

* * *

Coming to the corpse, Millard addressed his fallen partner, "Well Horace, I'm sorry it turned out this way. You were a fool to leave the dinghy. Your missing leg proves that. Ah, and now I have the map." Searching quickly, he found the leather, waterproof pouch, and then repeated his regret.

"Bercan, you wouldn't listen. I'll think about you when I bank the reward money." Millard spun around on his heel and started down the steep river bank. He believed the Kintu Falls lay about ten miles from the Bolango mine.

He pondered the thought aloud.

"I could be there by sundown, but I'm too tired. I can hardly put one foot in front of the other. I need to get some rest, right now. Then, when I wake up, I'll head for the mine. I can make the coast in four days, transact my business with BeMeers, and be on a ship back to the States by Tuesday. Huh, what am I doing: I'm talking to myself. That's a bad sign."

A single, ringing shot pierced the hot, humid, midday silence. High powered, the slug tore deep into Wren's left lung. Caroming off one of his spinal vertebra, it pointed at and pounded its way toward his heart. Once there, it sliced into the left ventricle and stopped. Millard took three meaningless steps and collapsed on the shore.

"We got him," Shields yelled, "The chase is over."

In half an hour the group came to the site. One man brought a shovel and began to dig a hole on the beach next to Wren. Shields walked over to the man and jerked the shovel out of his hands.

"Why bury the bastard? I'll cut off all his fingers. The blood scent will spread. We can leave the body on shore for the hyenas. In two days, only the bones will remain. You want to know something. No one identifies a skeleton."

Now it made sense: Shields vividly recalled seeing each man plummet over the falls. He knew what one of the two bodies might be carrying. He ordered the head guide to descend to the gorge floor. A steep rappel down the craggy cliff shortened his march. Adept at using a rope, the guide arrived at Bercan's corpse, first. Leaving the dead man as he found him, the tracker returned and gave his employer the details. Laughing, Shields chiseled a notch in his mahogany handled gun.

"Let Wren lead," he said. "Stay back; we'll learn a lot by watching." When a slug knocked Wren down, Shields dropped that line of reasoning.

Yelling, he said, "Who shot him?" He shouted again, "that was really stupid. What trigger-happy nitwit shot him." No one answered. They knew better. When they approached the area where Wren lay, the men all gathered around.

Dragging Wren's body into the next clearing, the men waited for Shields to suggest the next move.

"Son-of-a-bitch, why would Wren hang around? Maybe, he didn't have the map. Maybe Bercan did. That does makes sense." Walking closer, Shields said, "Search him." Upon careful examination, Bercan's pockets produced an oilskin pouch.

"Ah ha," Shields grizzled face brightened. "This is what we're after. It's the Bolango map. Boys, the journey is over." Swaggering past his men, he brandished the map.

"Let's get moving."

"Mr. Shields, please wait."

"What's wrong now?"

Shields' personal guide took off his water-soaked boot.

Soaked through and through the boot had been that way for days. The guide watched the greenish skin from his foot peel back. Alarmed, he yelled. The man began asking for assistance from Shields.

"Oh God, I think I need help."

"You'd better let me carve a little flesh off of your foot," Shields said. "It smells bad."

"Do I have gangrene?"

"Cripes, it's green, isn't it. Gulp down some brandy and call me in five minutes. You should be numb by then." In about the time it takes to walk a thousand feet the guide hobbled to where Shields was sitting.

Balancing on one foot, he leaned against a tree for support. Placing the man's foot on a log, Shields sliced open the meat. Inserting the knife, he pushed down hard. The toe dropped to the ground. Wiping the blade on a palm leaf, he had one of the men bandage the wound.

Still sitting on the log, he began to think about his partners. Shields became giddy with excitation. He thought about the reward. The shares were to be split 40-60. Then, he thought about the six men that might become jealous of him… But he did not have to worry. Discussing the split, they admitted that Shields had made it all possible. All the success they had worked so hard to accomplish was due primarily to the guides he had retained, and to the provisions he had bought. Shields knew that the group of men he had hired would travel best if their stomachs were filled at least once after the march through the jungle. Cheap corn liquor did the honors after each days' march.

One of the men spoke up in a slow measured beat, "We only brought ourselves. He should get the 40 percent. That leaves each of us with 10 percent." Everyone nodded their heads. They agreed the split was fair.

By noon, Shields' men stood at the Bolango. A hush settled over the group as they walked toward the large semi-hidden adit.

"That's strange. The entrance is wide open," Shields offered, "anybody with half a brain could spot the tunnel. Finding the bone buried in the tunnel may be another matter."

Unfolding the map, he followed the coarsely drawn lines, "Here's where they buried the bone. The map points straight ahead."

Entering the mine, Shields turned to the lantern bearers and bellowed, "It's too dark to see. Turn up the lanterns. There is no need to conserve now? This damnable hunting party is almost over."

Fifty paces brought the group to the Indian's femur bone as shown on the map. Shields, spoke in anticipation, "Hey, I think this is it. You there...bring the light closer, and hold it a bit higher."

Holding the lantern near the roof of the cave high, the hireling reached down and picked up the bone. As he lifted the heavy bone forty pounds of nitre-starch discharged. The explosion echoed off the walls of the tunnel. Glancing off the sides of the main entrance the shock reverberated dislodging three, huge supporting timbers. In clumps, sections of the ceiling fell to the base of the tunnel. Tons of loose earth and rock rained down on everyone in the shaft. The four lanterns went dark. Trying to avoid the avalanche of debris falling all around him, Shields tripped.

Falling backwards, he impaled himself on the sharp, femur bone. One short moan and he stopped moving.

No one saw the map's final location. Now reduced to shreds, it settled to the tunnel floor. Partially scorched, it left no clue as to the burial location of the diamond.

The explosion hurled the Impus Diamond forty feet further

back into the mine where it buried itself into a soft, clay part of the wall. Lodged six inches deep, it would be another time before the beautiful piece of carbon would find a new owner.

* * *

Chela, Oscars' wife asked quizzically, "Are you sure that was a dream?"

"That is one heck of a story. I'm married to you, so I know some of what you think. This tale sounds like a true story. In fact if I hadn't known your whereabouts for the last four years I'd suggest you had actually been there and did that."

"It's eerie, and it sounds so factual. Your imagination was working overtime when you dreamed up that yarn."

"The story does sound like the truth, doesn't it. I can't believe I'm telling this story to my wife. Maybe I'm going daft."

"I wouldn't say that, but it is a riveting tale. It's too bad. You're not writing a novel. This fable would give the average reader the willies. Seriously, I think you could sell the story in a minute."

"Shucks, are you sure you're not prejudiced? After all being my wife does put a spin on it that some stranger might notice."

"Look. Don't leave it there. Why not take it to a publisher and see what they have to say."

"Huh, you really think I've got a good story. It's original that's for sure."

"What can you lose? These guys are professionals, and the advice they give you would be a nod in the right direction."

"I'll do it. As you say, what can I lose. If they read the story line and think it's no good, so what. I don't mind getting a skinned nose. I've had them before. What's more, it might do me good. I need to find my way, back on the track. Somebody once told me when you grow out of your breaches its time to look in the mirror and decide who you are."

Oscar Fuller made the call. There was a good literary representative living in town. He had hauled many writers into prominence through his perseverance. Some authors had become very wealthy due to his efforts.

Oscar Fuller was not taking a negative for an answer. He secured an appointment with the gentleman for the following week. On Tuesday he entered the door of Mortimer Livermore. There was an exchange of greetings, and then Mortimer ushered him into his office and pointed to an over stuffed chair. Saying nothing, Emil sat down and handed a copy of the manuscript to Mr. Livermore. The man glanced at the cover, flicked through the pages, pausing now and then, to be more deliberate in his reading. Placing the printed pages on his desk he leaned back in his chair and chuckled.

"You have the makings of an interesting story. I've scanned enough to say it has a good chance to succeed. Of course it is in a rough state. For publication it would require a great deal of work. Also, you have no reputation on which to garner sales. This is a tough business. You just can't waltz in here and expect the literary world to buy your books. It isn't that easy. I assume you are ready to rewrite, again and again. I have had many fledgling writers walk through the door, but none have made the grade." He spread the pages again.

"Altering the subject matter is the first step. You will no longer be writing for your own tastes, you will be writing for the group that purchases your novels. I'm going to give you an example of what I mean. This poem was submitted by a young writer who felt he had talent. Here is a copy of that poem. Believe it or not I turned it down. That kind of poetry is not selling today. It's not because the poem is too farcical. No, it's because the proses are not in today's style."

Mortimer took off his glasses and wiped the sweat from his eyes and face. He spun his chair half way so he could view the street below. Then he softly began to recite.

Ideals, softly billowing, but they are silent.
Dried leaves stir in windless memory's eye.
An eerie draft of air, unable to relent,
Oft teaches human dreams to fly

A dearth of nature's music rides the currents.
Soulful, melancholy, but alas askew.
While choice, burnished fruit hangs listlessly,
Mindful of its fate, the human clue.

And so, in life, the labors of all women,
Live on, by some precarious thread.
Where heartaches are daily, rend asunder.
What comes is often more than dread.

"You know that by heart?"
"Yes I do."
"Why did you memorize it?"
"It did not take much effort. You see I wrote it."

There was an extended silence. It lasted for all of one minute, but Emil got the message.

Mortimer turned and spoke, "Mr. Fuller, I going to give you a recent submission to read from an unpublished author. Perhaps it will point to what I need from you. Today's story line must be more than a rendition of 'Once upon a Time.' That served to introduce beginning chapters years ago. Now, the average reader wants to be caught by your words in less than ten pages. Your epic does not start until page 70."

Mortimer opened a drawer and handed Emil about 30 pages of typewritten copy.

"Take your time, but read this essay with care. If you indeed want to write a winning novel this layout will act as a backdrop for all your future efforts. I have yet to find any grouping of words that handles the needed information any better. Do yourself a favor and make some copies of this, My guess is that you will be referring to it many times in the future."

"I'll take your word for it. The few sentences I have read, so far, grabbed my attention. Whoever wrote this had a grasp of what it takes to be a successful author. Am I right?"

"You've come close to the truth. I might even tell you his name. Does the moniker Percy Shelly mean something to you?"

"Yes, it does. Wasn't he a poet?"

"That's true. He was a poet. That's where he made his name and reputation. When he found that there were several writers better equipped, than he was, to write successfully, Percy switched to poetry. It was a wise choice. History tells us that Percy could not have picked a better venue to thrive in. As it turned out he was better equipped to write rhyme. If we read history, it tells the story. Mr. Shelly was a master at putting together good poetry. Go home and read this article slowly and remember the way in which it approaches the reader. Okay."

"Whatever you say, I'll be glad to do."

A hand shake signaled the end of the interview. Emil slipped out the door, and made haste to the elevator. It took all of twenty minutes to get home. Indoors, he found a quiet spot. There he slowly began grabbing at the meaning of this short undertaking. The written material began laying a clever background for the reader to absorb. Even so, the introduction took less than a paragraph. The feeling was strange. He had never read some unpublished writer's work before let alone a display of this type.

It shocked him to have uncovered these the feelings of a personality evidently buried in an adult mind many years ago. It felt even stranger to discover the subject matter dwelled on some explicit sexual words that five years ago had been taboo. Taboo in the public's eye, and on a printed page.

There had been a few authors who had defied the social norm, but they could be counted on one hand.

What kept the social departure alive was the success these writers enjoyed. Hundreds, yes even thousands of copies found their way onto the tables of the wealthy, and the avant-garde. With due diligence the literary commentary continued.

CHAPTER V

Some years ago, after hearing several views on sexual energy excursions, a friend of mine bothered sending me a short undertaking of a conversation which I quickly copied because I realized she had stumbled on the truth. The woman had received the information from a confidant who said, to her knowledge, it appeared to have been channeled from some spiritual being, and that she wasn't too sure she believed it or not, but to her way of thinking the information was surely accurate and that she thought she should pass it on if the opportunity came up.

Now, I endeavor to thank you for taking the time to explore this view point, and should you see fit, so to do likewise. The following is an inexact copy of her letter to me. I'm not at liberty to divulge the name of the author. I can state that the ownership of this information is not a part of my writing.

In reading this treatise, one begins to understand the enormity of the undertaking. Eyeing the message gives the reader an insight as to what is being proposed. Again, I only use the material for its impact on the young inexperienced mind. There are pros and cons to ferreting out this belief system, but all in all it's gutsy, and I think the subject will hold your interest until the end of the informative undertaking. The literary piece certainly lays claim to some long forgotten knowledge that uncovers the basic problems which confront mankind. Those of us who read the material sense the marked change in how men and women made love in the beginning, and may profit greatly by adopting a spiritual approach to the art of making love. There can be little doubt that some gross error is working its way through our society. Never before have there been so many dissatisfied women and men in these days of our highly stylized modes of living. Change, in how animals react to their environment, has been examined by pseudo experts, and other ill-informed scientists. When you include the human content in that analysis, it falls short of the truth.

We humans impart a grandiose understanding too much of the muttering of the professional standing on a Diaz intent on changing the basic laws of the universe. Socially, the only problem that most countries have is allowing those voices to be heard. Free speech is not to misinform audiences. Free speech is the right to pass on the result of years of effort, but limiting the right to say, "This is a truth."

So I begin by stating that the following may or may not be true.

Men and women have long since forgotten how to make physical love. This is the greatest tragedy of all time, for it is the cause of most of the unhappiness on Earth. This forgetfulness has been going on for many years. I might add. It is slowing getting worse. For years it appeared to be a natural problem. This means only individuals have any chance of starting to correct it. However, there seems to be no social solutions. The problem is too intense and too personal. Everyone has to discover the answer for himself or herself, or the truth cannot be accomplished.

A woman's ultimate unhappiness, her lasting discontent, is because the human male can no longer reach her physically. Her emotional excess, her depressions, her tearful frustrations, even pre-menstrual tension, and ultimately, the conditions leading to a hysterectomy and other uterine problems are due to man's sexual failures to gather or release, in love making, her finest, basic, female energies.

These extraordinarily beautiful, or heavenly energies are hyper-intensive and when left untapped in a woman, as they are now, retrograde into physical or emotional disturbances, and eventually, it is the woman who crystalizes into some form of physical abnormality. Yes, the womb is a battleground that gives birth to many different things. In all seriousness, some psychologists refer to the womb as a sexual spittoon.

Man's basic unhappiness, his perennial restlessness, is because, in forgetting how to make the right kind of love to a woman, he has lost his original Higher Power and, with it, sexual control of himself. His emotional, or psychic being, manifests itself racially as a sex obsession. All men, without exception are engaged in the tracking of sex!

Sex-fetish in man cause's compulsive sexual fantasizing, and uncontrollable masturbation, even though he lives with a mate. Sexual repression leads to anger, violence, and the universal symptom of losing himself in his work. Wealth-gathering, which compensates for a man's ineptitude as a true lover, also carries along. Business and wealth-gathering are cover-ups' in both sexes for the inability or the fear to love beautifully through the body.

Through his neglect for "love of a woman," man suffers from premature ejaculation, guilt anxiety, the self-doubt, impotence, sexual atrophy which masquerades as sexual disinterest, and sexual abstinence due to repressed fear of failure, sexual bravado and the lack of true wisdom. He inflicts all of this on women, thus aggravating her basic discontent and his own restlessness.

Every young virgin who mates with a man today is

immediately contaminated. His lack of love germinates in her the racial seed of discontent. She will be disillusioned. To be a fully integrated, male human being requires a man to assimilate through his body the divine female energies that woman can release to him only through restored physical lovemaking.

But the man has to be man enough, that is, has to be able to love her enough, love her divinely or selflessly enough during the act, to extract those energies from her deepest center. This does not depend on technique. It requires love, pure love. To be able to love this way is the authority man has lost, and his only true authority over the woman.

A woman, however, will not and cannot give up her divine energies to any man who is not yet himself, that is, not fully integrated or aligned, no matter how much she loves him and wants to give. As very few men on earth today are themselves, that is, they possess the authority to express and absorb sufficient love through their bodies to reach the highest part of a woman, the gap of unhappiness keeps growing.

The man who has developed sexual expertise still does not know how to make love in a Devine way. Heightened sensations and orgasms are gratifying and give him a form of authority, but these are not the love that a woman craves. The women or woman he makes love to, he satisfies, like a good meal, but soon she hungers again, and eventually despises her appetite, or herself because she knows she is not being loved.

In together relationships, the penalty man has to pay for his physical failure to serve women, as the personification of love, is her despotic emotionality. Wherever he loves or tries to love, she will one day shock this man, stun him, and devastate him by suddenly revealing in herself the fiendishness, the living female demon of emotion. She will show herself when he is attached and can't walk away. Any woman, who has not yet seen herself as a fiendish person, has not yet connected with her love.

The fiendishness of emotion in a woman is hell-on-earth-to-men. This is the part of her he cannot handle or understand because it is the demon of his own failure to love, to come to life, and so to scorn, abuse and torment him. He is terrified of it. He bluffs and blusters his way through, but finally, as he grows older in a relationship, the fiendishness will inevitably conquer him and force him to surrender the last vestige of his manhood and authority for the sake of peace. They will then grow old together, feeling safe but half dead as they lean on each other during the awful world of compromise. While the world continues as it is, the fiendish woman will never allow her man to forget his fundamental failure to love women in the right way. Women must be loved.

The future of this human race depends on woman being loved because only when a woman is truly loved can a man truly be himself and regain his lost authority. Only then can peace return to this disenfranchised earth.

Yet women as she is now, cannot be loved for long, or for good, by man as he is now. Together they are trapped in a vicious circle. And, if left any longer to their own ideas of love, there is no way out for them.

Love is in a dreadful mess on this planet. Something urgently has to be done. Any start must be made now, today, and you my friend must make it.

In these two short warnings I'm going to tell you how to make physical love again. But first I'm going to tell you about love and give you an understanding of the purpose of love, and your place in love and in life on earth. Love without a purpose, as you can perceive, in the world around us, is hopeless.

Understanding love as it is, and not as you think you know it, or like to imagine it, is the first lesson in making love.

I'm going to be straightforward and open. I will be describing the physical act of lovemaking in detail, using words like 'vagina' and 'penis' and other terms that lovers use. I'm going to be speaking very intimately to you.

I suggest you read these thoughts over and over again. Each time you will have new insights into making love. I suggest, you cannot be exposed to what is in these pages and not progress toward making divine love. You must absorb it so that it becomes part of you, part of your understanding.

However, test each statement with your own experiences, so if a statement seems to be outside your experience, listen for the ring of truth in it, the echo of knowledge you once had. That part of you, which is deepest and truest, knows all.

On the face of it, as far as I'm concerned, there is no reason why a child should not hear these words. I would like every boy and girl in their teens to hear the sentences over and over again as they grow into adults, especially the young women. Placing the information in the right vein is sorely lacking. The mystique has been missing from informal conversation for many years. Some righteous Elizabethan decided thoughts such as that should be withheld from the younger set. Few nominal Christians objected and the new rules slid down the spillway and were soon forgotten. Most of every life is moralized in that same way.

CHAPTER VI

The only problem is that when a child or a teenager asks intelligent questions, after reading the subject matter, will there be older, intelligent men and woman around to answer the query honestly and truthfully. That should be from a position of love and understanding, and of course, outside the vicious circle of society. I trust that will be so.

The main physical problem in lovemaking is man's premature ejaculations, and each woman, as I will explain later, unsuspectingly contributes to this untimeliness. Premature ejaculation is due to emotion caused by excitation and anticipation in both parties. This emotion, particularly in the man, is there long before any love-play or the physical act begins. In the man there is continuous, pre sexual excitement, or a rising aggression level due to his normal sexual fantasizing or sexual obsession. By joking and talking about sex with other men, by reading about it, by slyly alluding to it in mixed company, by thinking about sex, by looking at women in public and by making conscious and habitually unconscious lustful connections, he keeps his basic aggression level relatively high.

If you imagine man as a sexual thermometer, he is normally

registering about twenty-five degrees of sexual emotion because of his sexual obsession, while women normally are only at about five degrees. A woman is primarily less aggressive than man because she is not basically sex-obsessed. Consequently, man is ready for sex at any time, apart from his numerous hangups or inhibitions, where as women are not. For her to want to make love, her basic sexual temperature needs to be raised.

In the love-play before mating, the flirting, holding, kissing and fondling of the breasts and genitals, raises the sexual temperature of both parties. This added to the man's normal raised level of stimulation due to a sex obsession, make him fantasize far more intensively, than she. So again, his sexual temperature rises at a much faster rate.

By the time he is about to enter her, he is at a burning ninety-nine degrees, and still rising, with expectation and impatience. She is comfortable at an enjoyable seventy-five degrees, but rising too. Sometimes, she only has to spread her thighs to him: The final fantasy image is realized and he ejaculates or comes, or his penis touches her or just merely penetrates her vagina and he releases, or he just manages to make a single thrust and in seconds his sexual temperature drops form a feverish one hundred plus to nil as he selfishly backs into a rare state of cool, selfish subjectivity.

Woman, thank God, is the supreme expression of love. Love is her true nature: underneath all the emotions, notions, and hangups. If she loves him, or if she just loves, she can bear the sexual disappointment. Women at every level represent the mother, the true archetypal female. All of us delight and find pleasure in acknowledging her existence: even if it is only in a bottle of whiskey made out of the earth's grain and water.

Man, as he is now, is like a child to the boundless love in her, the true woman, which every woman underneath her neuroses knows herself to be.

In her love she can forgive him for that quick orgasm, nullifying her own desire mechanism, take his restless wordiness expressed in his own orgasm, and hold him there inside of her: boyish and new in his brief moment of peace. For a woman, the fulfillment of her love is to take him into her, everything he can give, while in return offering up every bit of herself in sweet, complete surrender to love. But the man when he comes prematurely was not in love enough to give her all of himself. He didn't have the time. So she in turn was unable to give him all the love she had to give. By coming, he went and left her unfulfilled. Because of it he is a little less a man, she is a little less her true self, and against the scale of man and woman's struggle to be united they are a little further apart.

A woman when she loves can dissolve within herself most of the frustration caused by man's premature ejaculation. Even so, any residual emotion from it becomes a part of the fiendishness which will crucify him on the morrow. But her love cannot compensate at all for the unfulfilled need to be relieved of her finer energies, to express or unload to man, in the love act, her intrinsic female beauty, the divine fragrance which builds up continuously in every woman and which is behind man's need for her. The pain of having to carry this unnecessary burden, due to man's default, is the deep grievance underlying the punishing moods and emotional fury of the fiendish female. A man who comes prematurely has temporarily lost the will to love, and has lost himself. Therefore he cannot take the complete surrender of a woman to her man and so is without real authority. He knows it, and is shamed by it. The only valid authority man can have over a woman is through love, and that authority she will concede to unconditionally when he demonstrates sufficient love to accept and take her to total surrender. Only when he can take her to total surrender, can the woman give all she can. His trumped up economic and physical authority over her, in the world, during the last few thousand years has been a nasty bit of work: that of getting even with her for his own weak abdication of his true authority. As selfless and magnificent, as a truly loving woman can be, the tragic division between her and her lover goes on from generation to generation, because man has forgotten himself, has forgotten how to love, and women cannot give of themselves, cannot reach her natural fulfillment without him.

The reason women do not fantasize about sex nearly as much as man is that sex is not as much a gratification to her. To a woman, sex is more love, and love unlike sex cannot be fantasized about. To love is to hold the still image of the beloved in the consciousness. One's fantasy starts as an erotic picturing: Sexuality and the sex shop take over from love.

To man, sex also can be love. But because he invariably uses it to ejaculate as a means of releasing pent up psychic aggression, and his sexual emotion, the act only contains a good deal of gratification and selfishness while he uses the woman. If he could mate with her without coming, he would start to love her rightly and for herself.

Ejaculation, as far as man is concerned, usually marks the end of the act. But of the woman, even if he has brought her to orgasm, he has still not collected her finer energies above orgasm: Her orgasm will release or disperse her immediate sexual emotion, but the higher divine energies that remain uncollected will finally degenerate into emotional demand and discontent. Sexual emotion in a woman is the demand, or cry, to be truly loved and not be used as a sexual spittoon.

At the beginning of time, when the world had just begun, the state of man and woman was very different from what it is today. When I say this, you must not confuse the beginnings of time and the world with the beginning of the universe of the earth. Let me explain.

The earth is not the world; man built the world. Time and the world began relatively recently about twelve thousand years ago when man identified for the first time with physical death. Before that time there was only the past, which extended back to the first life forms on earth. Time is not the past; time provides the sense of tomorrow or continuity on which the world was built. Before life on earth there was not only no time, but no past either-only the present, the presence or the timeless.

Time is not a process of things getting better, that's progress. Time is a process of things gradually getting worse. Things have got a lot worse for man and woman, or their love, since they started to slip imperceptibly into time or self-forgetfulness around 10,000 B.C. This you might say sounds like a myth; it is myth, but no myth as a fable or fiction. What I'm going to describe now, is the truth.

Myth, true myth, is the only means we have left of communicating fidelity as the original state of man and woman on earth. Please be as still and receptive as you can; suspend your critical mind and listen while I outline, for you, the myth or truth of man and woman, your own original state, in which you are striving to get back to by living and loving in today's times.

Originally, around twelve thousand years ago, the individual bodies of man and woman were permanently surrounded by a magnificent golden orb or halo. This radiating started at the solar plexus, and extended visibly to well above the head, into the ground and out beyond the reach of out stretched arms. The woman's orb was a slightly deeper gold than the man's, but both had the same dazzling, sublime and beauteous equality.

A woman is pure love: A passively serene, pole of human, spiritual love on earth. Man, the active, assured pole, also is love, but not pure love in the same sense. His was the love of pure authority, the masculine principle, which was the guardian of love, and of a woman on earth. He or his love was responsible for maintaining the golden, divine quality of love between them. The brilliance of their orbs or halos at any time reflected the intensity and purity of that love.

Their physical lovemaking was ecstatic. The divine energy generated was so powerful that after making love their bodies or halos blazed with incredible splendor. This self luminous radiance of spirit or love created in each by physical union was the manifestation of their Godhood on earth. Men and women, at the beginning of time, were gods, and they sustained the awareness and presence of their godhood, their timelessness, by making divine physical love. The halo or golden energy was their means of communicating, whether together or apart. Its realm went far beyond the visible outline, and through it each was in constant, undisturbed touch with the other, in stillness and in silence-that is, in mutual consciousness of pure love.

In time, when two halos need additional energizing, the man and woman will draw together, to make love as only two conscious, physical poles of love on earth, and so to illuminate or regenerate this love and authority.

Communication between them was so complete that there was no need for the voice of speech. Speaking developed with time. It developed in men and women, who by losing them selves in time, given to other things, to building the world, started to forget to love, that is, to forget how to be themselves, all the time. The result was they failed to make divine physical love.

Their halos or consciousness lost their golden connection and they had to start talking across the developing gap between them. Then, through speech, there arose misunderstanding and emotion. As time or lovelessness further invaded the bodies of man and woman, speech replaced the immediacy and fullness of love. Their vocabulary grew and grew. Instead of being that love they said, "I love you," and added many other wordy substitutes. Some individuals retained the intensity of the halo longer than others, but with time or the past increasing in everyone things got inexorably worse.

A few thousand years later, most men and women had forgotten how to be in love and how to make love. Although apparently exercising the same physical act, they were unable to release or generate divine energy and personify, within themselves, the living spirit or presence of love, the timeless love.

Man and woman's bodies were no longer aligned, in love, but in time and emotion. Instead of producing spiritually enlightened children, they produced emotionally dependant ones fraught with less than noble ideals. Theirs was the sin of an entire country and world. The commission to leave The Garden-of-Eden came shortly. Had they the willpower to resist the advice coming from the Dark Side, much, or maybe all, that has slipped into shadow would have survived, nay waxed strong in favor of Real Love.

The woman, who was once pure love, was now confused and perennially discontented. Man, having lost his authority, was now impatient with her, and, in trying to find a substitute for his authority, he became perennially busy and restless. Furthermore, lacking the authority to control her, he used his superior physical and economic strength to force her into an inferior social position, particularly by exploiting her love for her young children. This so enraged her that it engendered the fiendish woman, who as long as time continued would never forget or forgive his injustice and the corruption of love. For then, for the human race—the race in time had begun.

A few men and women, by deliberately refraining from making physical love, managed to retain a partial ability to love divinely and within themselves. These were the mystics, saints and ascetics of all nations. They turned their attention inward, and loved the divine energies in their own bodies.

By refusing to mate with other bodies, now filling themselves with time and emotion in the form of discontent and restlessness, the mystics kept themselves relatively pure. None-the-less, measured against the fullness and richness of original radiance, theirs was a pale and lopsided sort of purity. By denying the earthly need of union with the opposite pole or sex, the mystical alternative, for all its lofty devotion and idealism, was fundamentally and exclusively, unnatural and selfish. Consequently, it produced half integrated and only partly divine human beings.

As imagined, things were getting unmistakably worse. The result was reflected in the orbs and halos of these men and women mystics. Their halos gradually shrank in size and illumination, to a small circle of light around the head. You will see this depicted today in old paintings and icons, particularly around the heads of Christian Saints.

These shrunken miniature halos show just how restricted and formalized man's idea of love on earth, or earthly love had become, by excluding the whole of his or her body from divine union: Withholding from the opposite sex, on earth, and grounding love solely in the abstraction. Of the mind, the halo was reduced to encircle the head alone, or at least the upper part of the body.

It could be argued that the mystics and saints, due to the inrush of time, had no choice but to follow the way of celibacy. At least that way, they managed to keep some of the pure, divine love on earth, or until that sainthood disappeared under the weight of time. Many Christian's, because of their divine faith, felt the immediacy, the need for celibacy. In reality, the option they chose, not to make love, or their interpretation of that impulse was a great tragedy for the human race. The mystics and the saints just might have saved the day, or the world, had they acted differently or more selflessly.

Despite their divine love the celibate saints, like the rest of humanity, being swamped by time, had actually forgotten how to make physical love, but didn't realize it. They were very emotional about it. They even made a virtue of their forgetfulness. Perplexed and guilt ridden by the power of their own relentless passion, most Christian Saints fiercely denounced physical love making, and for all the wrong reasons. The truth is this: They didn't love enough. They didn't love their fellow man with sufficient golden intensity to dip into the divine mind with their own bodies, through intercourse, unable to recall how to make love on earth so as to give guidance or some sort of inspired example. That was just too much of a self sacrifice. So, like the mob which screamed 'Crucify Him,' they condemned the love they feared and did not understand.

The saints remained aloof from humanity. They were compassionate and mindful of the peripheral suffering of mankind, the poverty, disease, and violence, but always dodged the central issue of physical love. The Messiah, by his glaring omission of sexually from his teaching has a lot to answer for, doesn't he? That is if you believe his interpreters. The saints kept their hands clean, out of the real muck of love where ordinary men and women have to live.

"God is enough!" They said, "Is that true, if you are not a saint? Is that true for you? Or do you long to make love and perhaps sense something divine, pure and godly in it, which you know must be there and must be found? The saints abandoned us. They abandoned the blessed planet earth. They opted out of the reality of love on earth and made love to some other place where there is no need of love. Love is needed here on earth, and it starts between you and me, a man and a woman. Love is needed by God, who in that other place is the source of all love. I want you to escape to God in your love and leave the man and the woman behind."

"Then God must help us. You will have to return to make an amends, to see the error of your love as all the saints must do in time. Men and women need this love, this God of love. In the thick of it, here on earth, and not somewhere else where it already is and they are not. And only you and I together can make that love—that Godliness—here. It is this lack of love, or lack of God, between us that has brought the world today to the brink of annihilation by its own hand. Furthermore, these saintly, other worldly men and women loaded onto humanity, their own awful guilt. They believed that making love was sinful, a sin to burn in hell for. How many billions of innocent boys and girls and men and women have suffered hell on earth because of sexual guilt, and still do. Is this, the final consideration, having the courage to love the saints?"

"God, make me a celibate, but not today," Prayed St. Augustine. Why didn't he ask God to show him why he loves a woman so much he couldn't stay away from her, instead of praying for an intellectual ideal that just wasn't true? Where did he get the idea from, anyway, that he could be celibate-no doubt from some other self-tortured saint or priest? So the saints, mystics, and ascetics of all the nations abandoned the poor struggling mass of human beings who were fighting against time, and are still fighting to make love or peace with each other.

Did a saint ever tell you how to make love, which is the origin of all love on earth, even the love of God, for being all of us, even the saints, born of such love making? Is it intelligent to ignore the sweetest, most natural, physical feeling that two human beings can produce together on earth as signifying a possible reality?

Isn't that the obvious place to start looking for a divine love that we can all share, in saints and all others?

The saints tell us to love God, which no one on earth can possibly do by an act of his or her own will. How can you love-if you don't love? What sort of an exhortation is that? What would you say if I said, I feel hungry when you're not hungry? Or perhaps you've been told to love everyone. How can you love everyone? Can you possibly do it? Is everyone so lovable? Do you really love your enemies? Did you tell your child today, and not last Christmas, to love the person who beats them or punches them? Today when someone crosses you, can you see if you love them. Let's be straight.

Let's be honest with ourselves. We would all love everyone, but could we please start with our mate? Perhaps you will say that this is the task, to love everyone in spite of one's natural unloving tendencies. There's no task, no duty, no hardship, in loving. To try to love as a task is following the self shaming, guilt ridden, otherworldly way. That is not how to create divine loving. You start to love by making love, which is what you and everyone else on earth want to do most anyway. But you must learn how to love rightly, without self-indulgence, without seeking emotional satisfaction and self gratification. After you have learned to make true physical love and have started to restore your golden halo, you will then discover that you have found how to love your fellow man, how to love enemies, how to love God and yourself.

In very few women, is the upper half of the body, above the waist, integrated with the half below the waist. The top half, of the torso, where the breast and solar plexus are located, vibrates with a very fine energy of love. This is the finest love in the body. It gives milk to the child, and holds what is love to the bosom without the taint of sexuality.

This love is often felt as longing for the unattainable, the yearning for purity and idealistic beauty. It is the impulse behind the whole idea of Platonic love. This upper half of the body is the upper pole of love, the often sought after blessing that a Godhead bestowed on women, carefully preserved in some women for future reintroduction of divine love. Yes, it is still present here on earth, in abbreviated form, but active and waiting for the proper urging.

The lower pole of love below the waist is focused in the genitals, but the energy of this love is continuously present, though is normally discerned, in the lower back, the base of the spine, thighs, and legs. If you are very still, you will eventually isolate the distinct feeling of this energy. When perceived like this, without emotion or sexual associations, this lower love energy is felt to be just as pure as the higher love, only more grainy or tangible as a sensation. But that doesn't detract from its essential beauty or purity, for this energy rising through the legs of the earth itself, is pure vitality, or the life force before emotion as sexuality or sentiment has entered it. Man's function, as the masculine principle, is to unify these polarities of love in a woman, so that her whole system flows freely with divine love. For this union of the upper and lower division of the human body, that is, the ideal and the earthly, the unattainable, produce the single current of divine love, or the radiant golden energy. When this is achieved, women are reunited with their original true self, physically, psychologically and spiritually. Her discontent vanishes and she is no longer dependant on her work, art, motherhood, or any other external activity, to give her a sense of fulfillment or purpose. She may still engage in those pursuits, but no longer will be attached to them as a need. A woman's whole sexual motivation is to make the divine connection through man. Her desire to produce children is secondary and a substitute for the other. Because the divine connection is so rarely made, no woman today is really herself. She strays mostly in the romantic top half of her body, yearning for the unattainable and periodically or promiscuously engaging the lower half in sex in a futile endeavor to make the connection. But it evades her. So she remains virtually two people, divided in herself, until finally, cutting off from sex in disillusionment or old age, she lives a sort of half life of idealized love within her upper half. Frigidity in a woman is caused by lack of union of the love in her own body. It also helps to cause impotence in men, or his inability to have an erection. How these problems can be over come will become clearer as we proceed.

For a man and as woman of today to make love beautifully and divinely requires each to induce a fundamental change in the penis or the vagina. Both penis and vagina, or, more specifically, that part of the brain controlling them, has to be consciously liberated from the emotion or unconsciousness of the past, that is, from all habits, misconceptions and ignorance about making love gained through past experience. Experience "IS" the past. We can learn anything from experience, with the exception of how to make love. Love doesn't come from practice or experience. LOVE IS. The body doesn't have to learn how to make love; it makes love naturally. What we learn from the experience of lovemaking is not how to make love, but how to look after ourselves, how to safely and astutely project ourselves at the same time. This of course is a compromise; you just can't protect yourself, can't hold back in any way, and make love. But that is how everyone's love is made today.

With experience, the past has taught us to be cautious, not to give all of ourselves. We might get hurt, so we play it safe. Fear is very abundant. And in any case, we wouldn't know how to give our all in lovemaking anymore, we've forgotten that too.

Frequently people in love, feel the impulse to give everything, to want to tear themselves open, and yet they are not able. You must have had that feeling at some time. Would you be able to give your lover everything now, this moment if you had the chance? The answer is no! You have the chance each time you make love, and you haven't managed it yet, have you? Lovemaking today is a compromise, the acceptance of the best that we can be hoping for or done in the circumstances. And it produces at best for the lovers the finest feeling that men can be hoping for from compromised satisfaction, a poor substitute indeed for the glorious, continuous feeling of physical love made and given without self-consideration, without compromise, without holding the feeling back, without protection while expressing oneself.

This narcotic feelings of satisfaction which puts everyone to sleep after lovemaking is personified in the world by the male-made god of love orgasm. Man is orgasm-mad. And the woman, the goddess of love herself, infected and inflamed by the male madness, has started to worship this phony god, as if coming were a sign of love. Any animal can be made to come without a sign of love, but man cannot make love without love. So let's not fool ourselves or be fooled any longer. If you want an orgasm, go home and masturbate. If you want love, keep listening. Coming by man, before he has made sufficient love to collect the woman's divine energies, is loveless gluttony. Coming in a woman is easy and natural, sweet and becoming, if only the man and her self-protective experience would give her the chance too, natural and come naturally. But man, through his selfishness down through the ages and woman's gross trustworthiness, has taught, her, tricked her into chasing an orgasm, from the lovemaking he cannot give her. If you are chasing an orgasm, you can't be aware of the feeling of love. If you are a man trying to hold off an orgasm, you cannot be aware of the feeling of love. If you're a woman, and you believe orgasms are important in lovemaking, and you can't seem to have one, you'll feel deprived. You'll feel blame, or might give up trying to find love or an orgasm by turning your back on lovemaking, as so many women have, and again you'll miss the wonder and glory of love and yourself.

Woman, when she learned to no longer try to make love, when she is no longer lured or fooled by an orgasm, and refuses to mate with an emotional penis, when she is pure enough to be present as herself in the lovemaking act, without one thought in her head, will have an orgasm, naturally and effortlessly. She then doesn't have to try. It will happen beautifully, deliciously through the power of love, the power of the loving penis deep inside her. Today she can actually have an orgasm and hardly feel it. The ability to feel, the consciousness of love, is going out of the vagina. It is so ridden with past tensions and emotions that she can't get her awareness fully down there anymore, especially into the top half of her cervix. She has been virtually desensitized there, and it's getting worse with every generation.

Effectively, women have more pleasurable sensation in the lower half of the vagina than at the top. Because man can no longer get to the deepest part of the vagina in love, next to her spiritual garden where the true goddess of love resides, and stay there long enough to do what he is supposed to. He has virtually brought her feeling, and orgasm, down toward the front of the vagina. He has concentrated her awareness around the clitoris which is near the opening. He has done this in two ways: by persistently ejaculating prematurely immediately after entry and by persistently stimulating the clitoris with his fingers to compensate for the orgasm she does not have. He has gradually made clitoral satisfaction, clitoral compromise, the prize of love making. She knows it is not love, but what else can she do? What else is there? Further, because of man's failure to love her properly she sometimes masturbates on the clitoris as man has taught her. She wouldn't do this if she were loved. She doesn't have the same compulsion to masturbate as he does to relieve his sexual aggression. She got the habit from him. Only the penis, not the fingers or any other device, can love a woman. Only the living penis on a man's body is designed to serve the woman. Only the penis-a selfless, passionate patient, loving penis-can put the orgasm back where it should be, where it naturally happens or doesn't happen, without any disturbing emotions, because the woman knows by the feeling, the consciousness in her vagina, that she is being loved. Orgasm is an end, and emotional end. Lovemaking has no end. True lovers go on and on making love until finally, perhaps hours later, the man's body ejaculates naturally and consciously, or the couple pulls apart and make love hours later, or the next day, and the next, and the next, without the man necessarily having to come. Orgasm is a part of love making. But it is well and truly beneath the beauty and purpose of it, and it will happen rightly for both and without producing emotional traumas afterwards, if the two are present enough to concern themselves only with making love.

Most women's experience of lovemaking contains disappointment. Most men's experience consists of excitement at the prospect of ejaculation. Between HER underlying fears, reservations and hopes based on past experience, and his underlying dancing excitement, also based on the past, there is very little chance of real love being made between them in the NOW, the PRESENT. More emotion than love will be produced. By trying to repeat a good sexual experience, like coming, we make ourselves expectant or emotional. And by trying to avoid the repetition of a bad experience, we make ourselves emotionally wary and cautious. In neither case, can we make love. The astonishing truth which we don't realize is that the emotions produced in what was supposed to be lovemaking will surface in us within a few minutes, hours, or days, and cause a bout of depression or discontent, particularly in a woman. In man the emotion will surface as irritability, anger or aggressive behavior and he probably will release it further by masturbating. The fundamental change in the penis and the vagina necessary today to make love beautifully and divinely has to be brought about by the man or woman learning to become conscious, that is, to remain psychologically and spiritually present during the lovemaking act and the preliminaries. Today, due to massive accumulations of past references, and to the unconsciousness in their bodies, men and women make love for the most part in a subconscious, dream like state. What happens are their rising feelings of sexual love which excite their mental emotions? These emotions, the person's accumulated past experiences of sexual desire or longing, draw their attention or awareness back into the past as a fantasizing mood or image. Then being immersed in the past, they cut out as conscious beings from the love their bodies are making in the present. Psychologically they are absent from the event, no longer present, not there with their partners. They have drifted off into a world of their own.

You must have observed this by your own lovemaking possibly within yourself, but particularly in your mate. In those moments when you have been consciously present as you make love, and everyone is from time to time, you will have noticed that your lover has swooned off into a sort of personal euphoria. They are not with you, making love, here, and now. They are clearly absent from the present where you are. They have become self contained.

It's not common, in talking to someone, that you suddenly perceive they are not listening, that they are not with you anymore. They are miles away thinking about something else. In short, your lover has left you out in the cold, as it was. So you, rather than remain alone out there making love, endeavor as quickly as possible to get back into your own personal dream state, to lose yourself too in your emotional past.

You do this, and you will notice, through imagination, that by using sexual or erotic imagery, it again ignites the emotions. And off you sail into dreamland. Instead of the two of you being together in conscious physical union, which is the purpose of lovemaking, you are now dreamworlds apart. Lovemaking is self-orientated, self-indulgent and self-gratifying. Both of you in effect have borrowed the other's vagina or penis to make love to your own emotions, your own past. In such an insulated, but normal encounter, there is no conscious, timeless union of the male and female principle, no realization of consciousness or love itself, no union of the only two poles of godhood on earth into the one ineffable, divine presence realized as your own reality, the sublime, selfless spurt of love and life. Because more emotion or self is made than love, and since emotion or self invariably isolates, such lovemaking gradually pushes partners apart. They get sexually tired of each other and the magic vanishes. Lovemaking becomes habitual, a duty of an emotional release, not unlike an outburst of anger, and misunderstanding. From that, discontent and restlessness grow. The interaction of the penis and the vagina generates love. This love is the most intensely enjoyable sensation in the human body. Nevertheless, the intensity of the pleasure in love is severely reduced by the existence of emotion, or the past, in the genitals. The more emotion or past there is, the more numb and the more distant are the person's feeling or love and their perception of the love significance. Since every penis and vagina today is more or less infested with emotion over the past, no one suspects that the delicious body sensation normally felt in lovemaking is already deadened and distorted. Hence it does not occur to anyone to look for the naturally attainable ultimate, which is the incredible, direct feeling and perception of joy and love that are available to man and woman who can free their penis and their vagina from the past and so be conscious of the present, or Devine presence in lovemaking. It is toward this extraordinary, original human state of being and understanding that I'm endeavoring to lead you, and hopefully your partner. So I will say a few more words about feeling and the perception of it.

A penis and a vagina in becoming free of emotion, or the past, start to make ecstatic love together. The sensation and perception are so heightened that at first one can feel the possibility of losing consciousness, because the pleasure seems almost unendurable. As the process continues, one becomes aware of being completely present as the consciousness of the divine love is made. There is no limit to the wideness of being, and joy and the immediacy of the spirit that is known to the union, both by each, and by them, together, in the Divine presence. And because it is love alone and not emotion or imagination that is being experienced, and as love unlike emotion or orgasm has no end, the same rapturous physical and spiritual delight is present in all subsequent lovemaking together. In other words, the lovemaking does not vary; it has only ups and downs, no moods, no confusion, no personal or joint emotional disasters. It only gets better and better, finer and finer, much more Divine, and much more real, more conscious, more present, more astonishing and wondrous in its sublime perception of love, godhood and eternal purpose. But, as you will appreciate, this does not happen easily. A good deal of emotional and intellectual dying has to take place. It demands a lot of hard work on the part of you and even together, but the point is, it can be done. As we get down to the practicalities of making love, I want you to remember that the past is emotion, that when your words or feelings come from the past, from any moment before now, you are emotional. You are not straight, not to yourself, so you can't be in love or make love. Emotion, in fact, is the living substance of the past, the past living on in you. When you feel emotional, such as when you are resentful or depressed, you are feeling that substance, and you—are—that substance: That past, which is not you, who is listening to me, here, now in the present. The past, the excitable emotion trying to come back to life, takes over, and uses you. Also, please remember that the substance of every past sexual desire you have had since your teen's has lodged and accumulated in, your genitals, or that regal part of your brain controlling them. It gathers there as unsuspected tension. In women this tension manifests itself as a sudden tightness in the vagina, in man as a hardening of the penis, expressing itself as involuntary erections during the day or night. In both sexes this genital tension causes practically all the restlessness, heaviness and discontent. An emotional vagina, which is every vagina until it is made emotionless, or without the past by being loved beautifully and without desire, is imperceptibly stiff, muscled, expectant, self guarded, narrowly receptive and tense. A vagina used by numerous emotional penises starts to react like the penises themselves, becoming hard, greedy and predatory. It concentrates on the orgasm, but not on love. While being freed of emotion by a penis developing in love and consciousness, the vagina becomes, soft, giving, simple, easy, undemanding and still. The female organ of love is essentially passive and innocent. It learns all its bad habits from the male. The penis is the guru or teacher of the vaginas, for better or for worse. During intercourse, a vagina, made more hungrily by wrong penises, generates very little awareness of love for the woman herself, because the consciousness or pleasure engendered is based on temporary, emotional satisfaction. This causes her deep, inner unhappiness. Whether or not she is promiscuous, which is only a desperate search for love, is irrelevant. The vagina responds according to the energy of that which has previously entered it or informed it. Contact with a penis purified of emotion, or even one beginning to be purified, start the purifying process in the vagina. Even a virginal vagina today is relatively tense with personal past or emotion. This comes from the girl's sexual or emotional imaginings and related experience, which may include masturbation and male fingering. Here to, as soon as the virgin is pleasurably penetrated by the penis that is, when the pain of entry which keeps her temporarily in the present ceases-she will use this pleasant feeling to dream off into old imaginings and emotions and fail to stay with the wonder of the love being made by her vagina in the present.

The virgin vagina's basic tension, however, is due to the ignorance of love. Once, when time and humans were very young, each immature woman understood love because she was love. There was no ignorance of love in her consciousness as there was no emotion in her vagina. Her lack of physical experience did not cause tension because she understood love before having to make it, something we cannot conceive of today. She was free of the emotional ignorance of the unreal imaginings of love which all virgins today indulge in. Virgins today automatically speculate or fantasize about love because they no longer understand love or themselves. Also, there have been no real teachers, or gurus, on earth to tell them and instruct them before they receive the wrong impression through physical experience. With no understanding of love, virginal women start imagining what physical love is and that generates vaginal emotion, tension and hysteria.

Today, with so much racial past or time in the human body, the girl's vagina at birth is already potentially emotional. After puberty, when the virgin vagina is entered, informed or energized by an emotional penis, the girl's emotional potential is actualized, and of course then follows the usual predictable love problems between her and her man. Being in love without emotion, there are no love problems between man and woman. You must understand the penis and the vagina spiritually.

Both are spiritual organs and together are the means of all love on earth. If love is God, if love is our own godhood or the excellence of life then the penis and the vagina are the means of that excellence. Every man and woman, every perception of love and beauty on the earth, arises from the union of the penis and the vagina. Homosexual love, like all love, is an attempt to get back to the divine state where the male and the female principles themselves are united, the state of union that transcends persons and personal love.

The penis is the finest perceptive organ and knowing instrument in the male body. It has a consciousness and awareness of its own. It is the positive, active, organ of love on earth. It knows exactly how to make love and what to do inside the vagina. To make love properly, man has to learn to be his penis during the act: to surrender to its greater intelligence. At present, he forces his inferior, sex-obsessed, emotional intelligence onto it, with the result that the penis cannot do the job it's suppose to. Occasionally, however, in normal mating the penis consciousness is able to take over and the lovemaking is surprising right and good, but that is the exception. Most times, because the penis is used as an instrument of gratification for the man's sex obsession or emotional aggression and the woman's self forgetfulness, the love making ranges from satisfactory too mediocre through to a nonevent or a disaster. The vaginal cavity represents the emptiness in the woman, her eternal, racial longing to be filled with love. The penis stands for the only love that can fill it, and until the penis is there, man and woman cannot be content. The penis inside the vagina symbolizes the filling of the enormous gap that has developed in time between the two sexes-the gaps that created the world and through which the world continues to come to birth. The vaginal channel into which existence comes is then theoretically sealed; the cavity and its missing mass have found each other and are complete. Existence, as the search for union, by male and female wanderers is no longer necessary. But life as birth and death goes on: even if the union of the penis and vagina are doomed to separate, for above the place of union is the womb, and the womb will not allow man or woman to rest for long together on the face of the earth. The womb, or will, can never be filled in peace as is the vagina, for the womb demands birth, existence, and no rest. So, even as man and woman, the penis and the vagina, find rest and completion in each other, the womb above sucks into itself the seeds of life, and another restless missing part, another penis or vagina is born. The penis is happy only when erected inside the vaginal emptiness of a woman. When erected in the emptiness of space outside the vagina, the penis is impatient, excitable and emotional. In this unnatural state, it is naturally regarded by society as obscene and often by both sexes as threatening.

This is because the penis erected outside it natural vaginal home is a projection of aggressive emotion or imagination, and for any man, such an erection is demanding and discomforting. Frequently he will have to masturbate to release the pressure of its misplaced, lonely existence. If women's basic nature is love, what has happened to her? Why is she so often confused and unloving? How exactly does she contribute to her lover's ejaculation? How does she contribute to his impotence, his inability to get an erection? She does that too.

Over the millennia, man with his penis has gradually made women sexually like himself. He has induced, in her, a male-like-sexual emotionality, an alien sexual personality, that she can no longer distinguish from herself. Instead of remaining the pure and serene, passive, negative, female principle of love, under his sexual tutelage she has assumed a partial, positive, active, male stance, completely opposed to her true nature. Underneath she remains as a pure woman, as pure love—if she can reach down that far to her true self—but in her surface sexual projections, she is now part male. One result is that in leading up to love making her male emotionality gets excited like his. The immediate effect on her is negligible but on him it is electric. As soon as his penis makes contact with her body, these highly charged male vibrations rush from her to him as a wave of excitement and he ejaculates prematurely. The other male problem, impotence-not being able to have erections-is caused by lack of love or consciousness on the woman's part as well as the man's. Both partners are to blame. Behind this then is a crucial fact to remember: The penis is erected either by emotion or love. Without emotion, or love, it will not get to an erected state. This often happens when couples become physically bored with each other and have intercourse out of a sense of duty. If there is no emotional drive, as well as no love, no consciousness between them at the time, the man will not be able to have an erection. But if he has emotional drive yet no love, he will have no trouble getting an erection. An emotional penis does not need love to have sex, as every woman knows, but it will probably be a one-sided affair. The penis gets erected emotionally to gratify itself, to release the pent-up sexual desire or aggression arising from the man's imaginative obsession with sex. If the woman can get herself in the same condition of the mind, and she can, due to her artificial male side, they are able to gratify each other. But it won't be love.

Impotence does not exist in the sense of being a sign of masculine deterioration or deficiency. Many healthy young men suffer from impotence. Nor is impotency psychological in the way doctors explain it. Impotence is caused only by lack of emotion or love. So when a man gets older and living has knocked some of the emotional excitement out of him, and because by then, in lovemaking, there is so often no love in his body or in the woman's, he is more likely to be unable to have an erection. Impotence, or non erection, is the natural state of the penis outside the vagina. It is emotional, sexual aggression, but it is not love, that forces an erection outside the vagina. A penis responsive to love alone only gets fully erected inside the vagina, not outside in some imagined woman or mind-induced condition of excitement. A loving vagina has no difficulty in admitting a loosely full, loving penis, which will immediately become firmly erected for the purpose of love. However, and this can be important for the man endeavoring to purify himself: a pure and loving penis-is not able to get an erection if there is no love, or insufficient love, in the woman's vagina at the moment; that is, if she is dreaming off, emotionally distracted or sexually demanding. Such a man does not use the imagination as other men do. The loving man finds the moment, the present, the woman he is with, a sufficient stimulus. Purity of love is to be beyond the need of imaginative images and devices which emotional sex required. A woman has learned to make love through man who does not yet know how to make love. The result is chaos and confusion. Since time began she has been manipulated and encouraged to feel that the finest expression of her love is to please him sexually. The truth is, it's the other way around.

The finest expression of love is for man to delight her sexually. This can only be done when he can forget his preoccupation with orgasm and be sufficiently present in love or selflessness to collect and receive her divine energies, the finest expression of her love. By teaching her to please him and satisfy him down through the ages, he has taught her to desire him, to project herself sexually. This leads her to choose the man she wants. Desire and choice arise from male emotionality, the active outgoing principle which made the world what it is. So she chooses her man with her male-induced vibrations, and almost invariably, it's the wrong guy. A woman as her true self does not desire man. She doesn't need to. She is the passive, attracting principle. As her true self, she is like an irresistible living magnet, that without choice or error draws to herself the right man who will love her truly and divinely. Unlike man, a woman in her true self can exist without sexual intercourse or masturbation. She waits for love, not sex. Babies have long been her racial substitution for love in sex. The only reason why she started to go off into a dream in lovemaking in the first place was to escape his growing lack of love. A woman lusts after man only when she identifies with her enforced male emotionality. Nymphomania is an all male invention and projection, like sex shops, pornography and prostitution. The lack of love and male emotionality shared by all concerned, keeps them going. The woman has been utterly and sexually fooled by man. She has been pathologically brainwashed. And today, as she congratulates herself on progress in breaking down male domination in the world, she fails to perceive that he has got her as well and truly hooked as ever on his organic and clitoral substitute for lovemaking. Love, not equality, is what her external feminist protests are about. Male domination began in sex and in sex it continues unabated. It is a man's world and he built it on the strength of sexual aggression. But a woman cannot alter her position by merely withdrawing from sex or by using other devices. She has tried them all down through the centuries and none has worked and none will. The problem is now (way) beyond the personal scope of those involved to solve it. Only right action or consciousness can help.

We ask you, the women listening now. Has the female sex any idea of how to free themselves from male sexuality (dominance and humiliation)? Or, how can you bring real love back into your life? How can you make your man and yourself start to love, to truly make love? Anything tangible that you can actually create together is a start, as long you both are together? Well have you? If you have, please say it. Say it now, out loud or to someone before all. Say it now before you attempt it after I speak, to say you knew it all the time. Because if you do say that afterwards, you can forget it, you aren't going to change. You aren't going to make true love. To bring love into your sexual life, you are going to require a great deal of new energy. That energy starts with honesty, honesty to you and to life which is endeavoring to help you. First, you must hear yourself admit that your love life is not good enough. You must verbalize it, say it, hear it so that there is no hiding, no psychological escaping. It is not enough just to know it inside. That's how love dies between lovers. They think it's enough to know they love inside and not to say it anymore. Then when it's too late, they sob and scream out their love, but the door is already slammed shut, the house is empty.

You must say this now so that your whole being hears it. Second, if you are seeing the truth of what I have said about love, you must declare to yourself, that it is true. Third, you must admit to yourself that you personally don't know what to do about the problem, that you are powerlessly outside of taking all the old actions which human beings in their desperation and despair have taken quite unsuccessfully, since man and woman first fell in love, and time, or emotion, started to come between them. Be honest. If you already know the answer, why haven't you done it? And if you are hearing the answer, why are you listening to this message? Is it true that once you, both man and woman, knew how to make love? If you are hearing the truth of what I'm saying, it means not only that you are ready to remember again, but that you have already actually started to remember. And if as I go on you continue to verbally acknowledge the truth of it, so that your body or some other body hears your earnestness and humility, sufficient energy will be there in you to make a practical start. Such honesty and self knowledge generates passion. Passion is the power of love and true commitment. Passion is the only energy which is powerful enough to do the job. It's not going to be easy. You will use every bit of strength and self knowledge in your being. Remembering and acknowledging the truth as you hear it is one thing, living it or putting it into practice is the next thing. The living of it of course is what really counts, and that's hard. Nevertheless, if you have the courage, the self honesty, and want your freedom, your love, I will guide you into living it.

Please ask yourself these questions again: Is your love life, good enough? Is what I have said so far the truth? Does it have the ring of truth to it? Can you yourself through your own knowledge or efforts solve the problem? Do you need help? Examine the last question closely. If the answer is yes, say, "Yes I need help." Admit you can't do it alone, for when you give up, when you truly surrender in humility, help is always there within you, and then it appears outside you. Keep asking yourself the question each time you read this brief. Reaffirm the energy of honesty and true need. And as you put what I tell you into practice and see it working, acknowledge the truth of it. Keep the passion flowing with gratitude to love, and life. Otherwise, you will gradually forget what you have read and practiced, give up the fight and slip back into the vicious circle where nothing can be done. To start to make Divine loves, you again must first learn how to rid yourself of the past. You must unlearn or discard all you have already gathered emotionally. If you have had a broken love affair in the past, or a bad sexual experience, that motion will still be in you, especially if you are a woman. If you are a man and you study pornographic magazines or sexually suggestive pictures, that emotion is there inside you now, waiting to erupt and take you over in excitement and premature ejaculation at the first sexual opportunity. We are all sexually loaded, ready to go off emotionally as soon as intercourse is a possibility. But of course, we can't likely name or know all our past experiences associated with sexual emotion stretching back to childhood. They have all coalesced into one deep dark complex that is far too complicated and obscure for us to ever define. What do we do? We remove all the emotions from ourselves in our approach to lovemaking. We have to make love without the excitement, or expectation, or imagination. We have to be very much ourselves, very present, very aware, and conscious of everything we do as we come together. In what follows, I'm going to assume you have an intelligent partner, who read with you these pages and that you are both committed to endeavoring to make love in this new way. Also that you have decided to follow the instructions, adapting to them sensibly to your own particular situation, and not to give up no matter how hard things get or how often you appear to fail. Keep a sense of greater purpose. Remember, you must make love frequently, as often as you can, for only by making love, or endeavoring to, can true love be made. The less love you make, the more you grow apart. Further, you are going to be making love without emotion or imagination. The purpose of this is to get your habitual selves out of the action, for you to learn to leave it to the two bodies. At first, the lovemaking may seem strange, even cold. You might not get the idea at the first attempt, or you might get it right. If you do, you will have a setback sooner or later as emotion comes in. Don't be discouraged. Persevere. Keep going, keep loving. The connection will return or it will come suddenly and then fade out again as you go through another wave of separating emotions. You can't rid yourself of all the past at once or even in a few weeks. You actually have to work at it for the rest of your life. But all the time you will be making love, and becoming a much more loving and conscious human being. Some of these emotional periods may last for several days. During them, you may even tend to dislike each other. Lovemaking can seem impossible. Try when you can though, don't allow too long a gap. If, however, the emotion in either or both of you is too great to allow straightness or love, break off and try again the next day. But, I repeat, make love, don't make excuses. Put your bodies together and see. Understand that in the 'lead' up to lovemaking and in the lovemaking act itself you must have no thoughts or decisions independent of each other. Everything is done together and discussed and observed together as you do it. There should never be long spates of silence in the conversation. You must converse and verbalize constantly, expressing what you are feeling as your body sensations.

When you feel pleasure, say it, "That feels lovely," if it is. Say what you actually feel, not what you think. You are not supposed to be thinking, you are supposed to be being. That means looking inside your body at what it is feeling, not at what you are thinking. Communicate in words. This alone will keep you conscious and present in front of each other. Don't spread yourselves around sexually. Keep to the one partner once you find one. Emotional partners who are not committed will weaken you and make you lose faith. Conserve the energy. It is precious. Committed partners will not be easy to find. If you are currently without a partner, my advice is to only make love where there is enough love to begin with, and not just for emotional gratification or satisfaction on either side. Otherwise, wait.

When you meet someone and begin to like each other, be straight with them right from the start. Tell them the truth. Tell them you are endeavoring to love and raise your consciousness through love.

Take responsibility. Talk about what it involves. Read these pages. If you are serious and honest about loving, you will eventually draw to yourself a person who will share the start of this great adventure with you. If the partnership ends after a while, nothing is really lost. You will have both gained in love and consciousness and be that much more loving and straight the next time. The important thing, especially for women, is to be vulnerable to love, but to steer clear of emotion.

You know the difference now. Don't cut yourself off because you've been hurt. Be brave for love. Turn outward. Love will help you. Don't let fear harden you. It was emotion and lack of love that hurt both sides. It's past. Let it go. Now that you are beginning to understand what making love is about, you have the simple answer and the simplest protection of all: Make love only when there is love enough to be straight: And when it is present within each other, right from the start. And don't fall in love when you are in love. Falling in love is closing your eyes, shutting off your beautiful consciousness and tripping off into dreamland while you are awake. It is bound to end in disaster, because you will be in imagination and not see what is going on. But be in love.

Always be in love when you are in love. For to be in love and to keep love always fresh and new requires tremendous awareness, a tremendous presence of the kind that I have been describing on these pages. Be in love in this way and your love will not end, for love has no end. Fall in love and your love will end.

The two of you should decide in advance when you are going to make love. Allow ample time. No rush. No available distractions. It is imperative that the woman sticks to her decision to make love. If there has to be a time lag, due to work, or children, she must make it clear to the man, that when the agreed upon time approaches she won't have a headache, or not feel like it, or be too tired. She must take responsibility for herself as he must for himself.

Her declared position must be. I'm going to make love with you. There's no reason to be impatient or doubtful. I won't change my mind. Otherwise, as the time approaches he will start getting anxiously excited and impatient. He can't help this when there is any possibility of delaying lovemaking. His deepest subconscious fear is that she will change her mind, and that for some reason he won't get there. Excitement comes from anticipating an end, to this an orgasm. And he has yet to learn that making love is not an end, not an orgasm, that when he can make love and go on and on, you, his woman, will be available all the time and anytime. Who's not available for love, only those who do not know? So, in the mean time, the woman has to consciously dispel his mounting excitement by reaffirming her availability. It is the woman's implied unavailability that excites man and makes him hopeless as a lover. He then desires her instead of loving her, and desire soon runs out, or tires as every woman who has excited a man discovers. Of course, if your physical relationship is an old and weary one, the problem won't be excitement but being able to be new, to be refreshingly present every moment as your bodies face each other. Making love as I am describing it will give you both a new approach, a new energetic interest to find out if it works and that will help to keep the old habitual selves out and allow the present to come in. You didn't have to worry about feeling like making love; that's an emotional red herring. The bodies, love to make love. The part of you that feels like it or doesn't feel like it is the problem. It's the emotional thinker that gets in the way. Leave it to the bodies and they will make love. Stay out of it as much as you can. At the start, especially if the man suffers from premature ejaculation, the woman is likely to be the stronger or straighter due to her innate lack of sexual excitability. She is likely to quickly grasp the spirit of what her man is endeavoring to convey. She must keep the man straight by seeing that he does not lapse into imagination, for without realizing it his mind will start to throw up erotic and sexual pictures or thoughts that have nothing to do with the woman he is with. She must constantly work at keeping his sexual temperature down. But she, too, due to her acquired male emotionality, can quite suddenly get off balance, particularly if she is near her menstrual cycle. Her period, through it's a racial association with men, exploitation of her, through her young life, makes her ultra defensive and suspicious of man as well as herself. Her female perception is heightened and, as this conflicts with her male emotionality trying to project out into man's world, she often becomes confused and unsure of her role at these times. He, for his approach, must keep her straight too. He must be alert to see that she stays present. But neither must accuse the other of being emotional as this will generate more emotion. If one suspects that the other is emotional, and not being straight, he or she must ask the other questions, "What are you feeling right now?" Or is this true now? Always refer to now, not to yesterday. If each answers honestly, and stays present as they are committed to do, the emotional ones will see themselves as emotional, and, by admitting it without argument or justification, the emotion will tend to dispel and love will be the remainder.

You must keep talking. Always to the point of what you are

both doing and feeling now. You must not dream off. You must keep in the present.

You will soon get the hang of it. Trust each other, hear each other. Don't be upset by the other saying that you're not present. Resist the urge to argue back. Listen. Discover things together. There is nothing to defend if you are straight.

Let us say the time has come when you have agreed to make love. Undress in the same room. Keep the light on. No hiding. Don't be concentrated. Love is a serious business, but it is not that serious. Look at each other, eyes and body. Smile. Don't think about what's going to happen or what you're going to do.

Be in the room there together, now. Stand naked and apart. See each other's bodies, no judging or thinking, just staying in the present. Please don't be self-conscious. Hold to love. Start by loving yourself and being yourself, blemishes and all. If you see your partner is self-conscious, help them. Smile. See something really truthful to say. Look for the beauty of the being within coming through the body.

It's there. See it. Be innocent, be new. Don't look back. Be yourself, just as you are now. Be naked psychologically as well as physically. Be vulnerable. You've got nothing to lose that wasn't lost a long time ago. While you are looking at each other, truly seeing, without using your imagination or trying to jump into your next move, you can't think, can't use the imagination-which, if it can, will project into making love to someone else or an imaginary vagina or penis that's no really there. Why do you need the imagination anyway? Is it to get in the mood, to get an erection? Nonsense! That's an emotional habit most of the world has got into through lack of love and understanding. It's a very difficult habit to break, but you've got to do it. We can do it together, if you will stay with me in the present. You don't need your imagination to make love because you are with the real thing, the actual living man or woman who is going to give you the most delicious, pleasurable feeling that you can have-in the flesh and not just in the mind. Can you see now, how we've all been hoaxed by imagination? How down through the ages children and adults have ben masturbating and making love to imagination, unaware that the imagery, not the action itself, is utter self delusion, and cruel addiction? And because everyone indulges in the same imaginative drug, its loveless escapism is considered normal and even necessary with being considered at all. Let me anticipate a question that will be rising in many of you, especially the men. How do you masturbate without imagination? You, the adult, can't. When you cease imagining, the masturbation stops. The imagination is the habit, not the masturbation. The imagination arouses the emotions and that drives you to masturbate. If you have to masturbate, and due to male emotionality the pressure to do so is intense, particularly in the male, use as few images as possible. Don't use faces. No one ever made love to a face, except in imagination. You are a man, use only the image of the female partner. Get the images down to that alone. That's the closest thing to the actuality. Wean yourself in your head by not thinking or lusting in normal times after the opposite sex, and the impulse to masturbate will gradually disappear. Start now by giving up the universal drug of sexual imagination. Be yourself. Be where you are. Be responsible. However, don't feel guilty if you do masturbate, nor allow your children to feel guilty. The guilt of it distorts the personality of both the young and the adult. The error is not in the act of masturbating but in the misuse of the imagination-not only during the act, but more importantly during the rest of the working, reading, thinking, and socializing day.

The compulsion to masturbate is racial. It is part of the evolutionary past, the unconscious, projected male drive of the animal species from which we derive, and which mates mechanically or instinctively, solely to reproduce. The male monkey masturbates with outrageous detachment and lack of guilt!

Unlike man, he couldn't care less. That's because he can't make love. If the monkey had the creative power to make love, he would see himself masturbating and feel wretched too. But his only option is to masturbate or reproduce. The power to make love, which man alone possesses, is the self consciousness which distinguishes him from the rest of the animal species. When, however, through sexual imagery he misuses his otherwise unique, creative gift of imagination, he taps back into his animal past, into the mechanical animal drive, and masturbates and mates without love. He is then not happy. Until man has made sufficient love to replace himself on earth, he can never be happy.

Have you lost the urge to make love while I've been talking? Not really, the body doesn't lose the urge to make love. It will always enjoy making love if the monitor, you, doesn't get in the way. Smile at each other and embrace, still standing. This is the time when the imagination is likely to start, when you're looking over each other's shoulder or when you close your eyes. Let no eye close. Feel each other's flesh, back and arms. Don't think— feel.

The man can caress and fondle the woman; she can caress and hold him in love but not fondle his genitals. She remains passive, responsively undemonstrative. It is his job to please and delight her, to give to her and not to excite himself. He must focus only on pleasing her, and that will give him pleasure without emotion. Gentle kissing on the lips and torso is okay, but no tongue kissing. The tongue can be like an emotional penis, lovers lose and hide themselves in such kissing. Love is made consciously in the vagina-you are not there yet. There must be no substitutes.

When you are there, and have learnt to be fully present you can do anything your mutual passion requires. At this time, keep each other present by saying what you are feeling out loud. If you feel passion rising or excitation, say it. Put your attention on the solar plexus, for that's where passion starts before spilling over into the genitals. The woman probably will be able to feel the solar plexus before the man; in his excitement he is likely to miss it and connect up with emotion in his penis. Smile, make a joke if you feel it helps. Perhaps you feel that making love like this is as clinical as a visit to a doctor. It's true. That's how it's supposed to be, until you break through. Stay with me please. It is possible the man will not have an erection or may or may have lost it.

If he has lost it because of lack of imaginative stimuli, it is a good thing. By continuing that way, he is less likely to ejaculate prematurely when he erects inside her. Or he may have become so dependant on imagination that without it he can't get an erection. This is more if your past lovemaking has been habitual. Remember, an erection is only necessary in the vagina where love is made, so he doesn't need an erection at this stage. If he has a full erection now, he is emotional and already on the way to a premature climax. But he should not feel disheartened if he does have one, he has just got to try to keep any more imaginative stimulus out, so that his excitement doesn't become uncontrollable when he enters the woman. She must remind him continuously so he can keep breaking up, interrupting the force of his desire, and keeping his sexual temperature in check. If the man loses or half loses his erection, he can afford to kiss her breasts and fondle her genitals, but without finger penetration-in other words, show her love, in his hands. He does not require an erection to feel passionate and loving and to inhale the spiritual fragrance of her feminine presence. As he loves her like this, her passion will be rising. While she works at keeping his imagination in check, he must be alert to see that she is really present, especially if she is enjoying being fondled. They must keep talking, always to the point of what each is feeling now, with no long silences, no blissful euphoria that isn't verbalized and shared with each other. If the feeling is sweet, beautiful, nice, lovely, whatever is the right word, she should say it, His job is to love her by pleasing her, and she must respond and acknowledge his loving. However, she must be careful not to just observe the feeling she has. She must aim to be that feeling, to get her consciousness into that part of the body where the pleasure resides. At this point, after minimal and occasionally not playing at love-play at all, the two of you should lie down together and the man should enter the woman gently and lovingly. The idea of minimal or no love play is to enable you to realize as a new, conscious experience, that of the penis and the vagina together, and nothing else, are what makes your love. Everything outside of that is imagination and an avoidance of the responsibility of love now. This is extraordinary, a simple truth that men and women have forgotten, and they show how they have forgotten it by continuously being carried away by imaginative substitutes for a love that never works. No matter how many delightful love stories you read or hear, or how many sexy movies you see, or how much love play you engage in before intercourse, every time the magic and romance between you and your lover will still inevitably fade away. All those substitutes for love dull the perception and prevent you from staying with and facing the simple truth, the reality of now. Let me tell you very briefly how physical love play originated, and you will see that it had to do with the start of imagination on earth and nothing to do with love or lovemaking. Love play evolved in the species, as you can see in the mating game played by nature's creatures, long before creative man appeared on earth. They were natures' way of introducing the first vestige of imagination into the developing animal brain, which was to eventually evolve into the human brain, your brain. Nature's mating games, as you can still experience in your body today, caused extended pleasurable feeling in the primitive, unconscious creatures without any love actually being made. And the constant pressure to increase the awareness of that good feeling in time produced the first signs of instinctive mental activity or imagination in the brain. But man, who entered the physical body or brain prepared for him by some amount of change around twelve thousand years ago, is a spiritual or creative being in his own right. He has no need of the lower-self-based or sex-game, based animal imagination that is a part of the brain's historic past. All he needed was the final superb instrument, the human brain, to allow him to exist and be in the present. At first, he had little trouble resisting the brains instinctive game-playing imagination, and bringing to earth the new order of spiritual love and divine presence between man and woman. But gradually, with the accumulation of time as I have described, he and she reverted more and more to primitive, imaginative sex games and forgot how to love. The truth is, and if you can see it, will be a mighty moment in your life. For a man or woman, who are being themselves, in all the normal, social flirtations and passionate, private petting preceding lovemaking, can still be a way of avoiding taking direct responsibility for love now. For us, but not for the animals who can't know better, such love games are like having to take a stiff drink of whiskey. Or a dose of the wrong spirit, to try to get our courage up, or a drug to help us forget what we're doing, because we're not prepared yet to be ourselves. We have to face up to the reality that love is made now, not at some future time.

So, as is usually the case, in this manmade world, the reverse of what is accepted and practiced is the truth, the world does play games and doesn't make love.

The plain truth is this. Make love and don't play games. As you come together now, I want you to be detached emotionally, that is, detached from the old brain, the past, but present in love, aware, patient, considerate, giving, and able to see the funny side should that occur to you.

If the man doesn't have a full erection, he may have to be helped into the vagina. But if possible, the woman should avoid stimulating by fondling. If there's sufficient love between the two of you, he will have enough of an erection to enter.

It may be that he will have to lie there against her until the love comes through. It can't be hurried or forced. The same is true when a man is apparently impotent-there's just not enough love present and you must both wait patiently, or get up and try later or the next day. You are switching over to love as the guiding power and must have faith in it. As soon as the love flows while you are lying face to face, the penis will suddenly move like a living thing and extend toward the vagina. This will amaze you, particularly the man himself, and you will begin to understand the wonderful power and intelligence you are endeavoring to connect up with. Once inside, the penis, given the presence and love in both partners, will always become erect in the vagina without stimulation beforehand. Then, on future occasions as you both persevere in this way, you should be able to make love for lengthening periods to your mutual love and delight. But on entry now and in the future, the man must be prepared for the down-rush of women's male emotionality. This will make him come, sometimes to his astonishment or puzzlement, with the penis only partly erected. The more she learns to stay present, and to be united with the consciousness or pleasure in her vagina, the less release of this energy will be a hindrance to him. During entry, nothing should be forced. Gentle firmness is the way to love. After making love consistently in this way, the vaginas will become more sensitively receptive without needing external stimulation. I give you a word of caution. Only emotional tension makes the vagina resistant and not ready for love. As the emotional tension is reduced, which means the consciousness or sensitivity of the vagina will be increasing, so the woman's joy in lovemaking will grow. At the same time, the man, as he leaves emotional dependance behind, will grow in presence and begin to feel a new sense of command and authority coming into his life. Remember, if a man before entry has a full erection, he is already emotional. This is normal today, but means he has to be very aware and still as he enters, or he will ejaculate. A penis erected outside the vagina has an emotional will of its own. Inside the vagina, that powerful will, can enable a man to suppress a climax for several minutes. But as suppression is not love, the lovemaking will not be satisfactory to either party, unless it is one of those times when everything comes together. He must enter her slowly. As he does, he must be one with the feeling of the penis, that means he must feel what his penis is feeling every moment and not just the urgency, the pressure of his own desiring. He must get to know the difference. He must get his consciousness down there, into his penis where the love is being made, and out of his head.

He must not allow his mind any fantasy. He must stay present without imagining where his penis is. His penis has no imagination, only the feel of what is, where it is. He must be that feeling: The ultra-sensitive consciousness, which responds in perfect harmony to the energetic needs of the vaginal consciousness. One thought about where his penis is and he lis likely to ejaculate. The moment he feels he can't stop himself ejaculating is the moment he can. He must not believe that first feeling of the inevitability of orgasm and give into it. It is a trick of the pent-up emotion wanting to be released, which is part of the old animal drive to masturbate or reproduce. When the feeling comes, he must cease all movement, be completely still or withdraw immediately. He will discover which is best for him. He must not give into the feeling. This split second is crucial as it marks the point where he can use his creative, spiritual authority, or presence as man, and resist or dispel the instinctive animal emotion. I repeat; he must not go with inevitability, he must not believe he's unable to stop, because he can. Only in that next instant, is the orgasm inevitably cast. On entering the woman, with an erection, he should penetrate as far as he can and lie still. He should allow his penis to feel her, to absorb the vaginal energy. It will inform the penis of what to do, what is needed. He must respond only to his penis, not to what he has learned, heard or can remember. He must keep the past, all past experience as thought, out of it. He must be, as new, as the moment itself. Then the penis will do its divine work. She must make no movement with her body that she has learnt from other lovers or acquired through reading or watching films. All movement must be left to her body, even if it means no movement at all. In the beginning it may not be easy for her to separate the two. The contrived body contortions making phoney signs of pleasure and participation, of the pure, imperceptible, natural movements of her body come under the control of the vaginal consciousness. Later the body will move passionately, but not necessarily demonstratively, like any male like assertiveness or aggression, are suspect and have to be abandoned. She must remember that love in women is not a projection. It is a still, quiet, natural, flowing motion. Flexing the muscles of the vagina is a good trick, and is sure to entertain an emotion; penis, but it is not love.

The couple should continue to keep up a loving dialogue of what they are feeling, each saying how beautiful it is and how much they love making love, if that is true. Making love is beautiful, and everyone benefits as the vagina and penis become honest and free.

Instead of being in a hurry to move backwards and forwards, the man could endeavor to stay near the top of the vagina. The vagina is an emotional cavity fraught with hidden tension: Each time the head of the penis should open it up, taking the strain, and residual emotion out of the whole upper and lower half by moving as far as possible, from side to side. As the man becomes sexually still and present, the head of the penis acts like a highly sensitized magnet. First it gathers the vaginal tensions, provided she is learning to be herself and not to project them as needless activity, emotionalism and personality.

Then the penis begins to collect her Divine energies. When the divine energies have been gathered, the purpose of lovemaking is served and the man may lose his erection inside the vagina without having an orgasm. The need to control the birth rate on the planet arose only because man lost sexual control of himself, releasing sperm even as he got an erection outside the vagina, and ejaculating inside as a matter of course. When time and the world were very young, and man and woman made love consciously as the gods they are, to be present in a body on the earth was a great privilege. And the population, due to man's responsibility to love a woman, was kept very small. Men did ejaculate in lovemaking, but very rarely, and then only in the moment as determined by the Divine intelligence, the love itself, with which he was united.

Today, by right loving, and being the feeling in the vagina or penis, and not trying to hold to an aloof position, sexual identity which is (self) the man or woman will in time get the consciousness of love that is behind the part of the brain controlling the genitals. Here, the two poles of love on earth, the masculine and the feminine, are making the magic of consciousness, the Divine presence of their mutual godhead.

Love or God can never be the subject of a philosophic exercise. Love or God is too real. Love or God is loving and doing now, not speculating about it, not thinking about it. In these few pages I trust I have not been philosophic but pure and down to the blessed earth, so that love and God are truly served in some understanding—not only when you are making love, but now when you have the opportunity to be all the love you have ever made. For now is every moment. Let me finish by referring to romance. Romance is not a passing thing. Romance is not a box of chocolates, anniversaries remembered, sweet words, pretty things, love letters or beautiful evenings together. These are a part of the romance of living, and so we come to death which spoils it all. You can't have the good without the awful shock in the romance of living.

CHAPTER VII

True romance is the myth of life, the stupendous adventure of man and woman together, discovering though love, and though each other that there is no death, no end to life or love that does not hold a fear. IN THE WARMTH OF LOVE I LEAVE YOU. IN THE BLAZE OF A NEWLY FOUND MEANING REGARDING SEX, I BOW TO THE ARTICLE YOU HAVE JUST READ,

* * *

Lorraine and George looked longingly at the clock. It was 6:30. Dusk had already settled in. It had been a long day. For three hours, the questions pertaining to the problem in the nursery had been coming thick and fast.

Lieutenant Baldor leaned back and addressed the elder, grey-haired Sargent who had been taking down the information in short hand.

He said, "Maybe we should quit. It's late and the witnesses are getting a little uptight. We can finish Monday. We should be well rested by the beginning of next week"

The group nodded in unison, and Baldor waved them out the door.

The following morning, St. Mary's Hospital was buzzing. News of what had happened became common knowledge throughout the city. Several papers ran two-inch high headlines. An article, by a line reporter, appeared in the local newspaper. A copy was placed on every bulletin board in the city hospitals. An artist's concept of the offender also appeared in the right-hand corner of the notice.

The body of the article stated, "Be on the alert for the person pictured above. He entered Saint Mary's, New Born Area and switched six babies from their assigned beds to other beds containing different names. None of the infants were over a week old."

When the news leaked out, frantic parents began trying to identify their babies. They found it impossible. Then the police handed out a communique: A man dressed in black was seen leaving St. Mary's Hospital at four o'clock on the morning of April 10, 1999. Any information you have might help return the babies to their rightful parents.

CHAPTER VIII

Another reporter's write up of the crime appeared in the morning paper. The article claimed that the night nurse had found a letter explaining what had taken place, and that the culprit was asking for a large ransom. She left the hand written ransom note at the admission's desk. It stated that the man claimed he could restore the proper order involving the babies even though the arm bands had been removed. That forced the hospital to admit they were unwilling to move the babies from the position they were found in on Friday morning.

The hospital responded by offering a sizable reward. The reward stated, that the hospital was seeking information which could identify what baby belonged to the right parent. The cash award was sizable.

Sister Sarah stated, "We are willing to pay a handsome stipend to end this grief. I will tell you the money will total six figures. It is felt that a cash reward of this magnitude would bring an end to the distress of the families."

Fathers and mothers, after hearing of the reward began showing signs of a mental imbalance. St. Mary's pharmacy handed out several bottles of anxiety relief pills to ease the strain on the parents.

One gentleman, the same reporter from the local newspaper, spoke his mind, "Can the people ever know the truth? How will the hospital return the babies to their rightful parents? The only real hope is the new DNA analysis. Even then the parents will always have doubts. I wish them the best of luck. This is the most frightening thing that has happened since I joined the newspaper. Being a reporter, I've covered the good, the bad and the ugly when it happens. In this town it doesn't happen very often. What spineless jellyfish would do such a thing. I can imagine how the parents feel, never positively knowing that the child they wind up is really their own?"

A sobbing parent spoke up, "The shame of it all, to suddenly know that our city has a person living here that would stoop to such a unholy act. It makes my skin crawl. I for one want the person caught and either hanged or run out of town on a rail. I'm sorry, I won't feel comfortable until this is over."

She turned to her husband and spoke, "I went to bed last night and prayed it would all turn out for the better. Nevertheless, I haven't slept well since it happened."

"I believe the hospital has learned a lesson. The older type surveillance in the delivery ward will change. You can bet the latest equipment will become more prone to catch anyone who stands outside the law. Even the person, captured by the police, will be dealt with much more harshly. In the past, prison sentences of this type carried a sentence of ten years. They would now increase to at least twenty years. The judgment would include incarceration without parole."

One of the Judges of the court wrote a paper defining the reason for the mandatory sentence.

We have gone to great lengths to make our society a better

place to live. Babysitting, law breakers, is now to the point where they believe that any jail time is really a deserved vacation for them: Three squares a day, a roof over their heads, and nice clean clothes is their right. It's much more than they deserve. I for one, want to put a stop to this permissive behavior.

In a loud voice he spoke to his audience, "Our society needs to understand that the visitation of freedom does not give licence to unwarranted actions by the citizenry. It smacks of an uncaring group of Hedonists."

A television moderator from England reminded the Americans of their personal cliche concerning the financial attitude held today by the public. I think he told it like this. 'I've got mine, up yours.'

Indeed, the moderator suggested it was not a laughing matter, but the audience roared its approval.

The reporter spoke harshly, "Not me, I was embarrassed, so from now on I will treat unlawful conduct as it should be treated. There are no shortcuts to good social behavior. One should practice the edicts laid down by our parents, or by the books they read on proper convivial discipline. Our society has erred on the side of ignorance too long. To our regret, we have followed the errant side of every school of higher learning, and much to our dismay the walls have come tumbling down. Woe to the purveyors of liberal education, where Darwinism has taken the place of common sense. All too soon the band begins to play and like the fairy tale, the average citizen follows the Pied Piper down to the river of flames to their untimely demise. I find it hard to believe that so many, go so willingly to their end. They go without examining the pros and cons covering basic facts. Government institutions, and teachers, in today's educational establishments have reduced the three, 'R'S to some outdated ritual placed on the shelf, to be referred to only when a bothersome question by some indignant parent arises."

The judge added to the indictment, "It's a sorry time when we have to wait until disaster strikes before the penal institutions respond, but it has always been that way. America is a reactionary country. We wait until some devilish thing happens before we take action. Maybe it's because those in charge have no vision. By that I mean they find it impossible to anticipate trouble and thoughtfully take measures to guard against that trouble." He stroked his chin apprehensively.

"However, I'm quite positive that future mothers will not have to worry about the safety of their babies at St. Mary's. The hospital has already installed new hardware locks with combinations known only to the medical personnel who work there. Each of these people has special clearance. I know that for a fact."

A man in the audience asked, "What does it all mean? What's happened to the ethics that citizens once lived by? Is it our new attitude?"

"I think that's it in the nut shell? Let me explain."

The reporter whose article was the focal point spoke, "No, you let me explain."

For a long time, I've been unable to sense my feelings correctly. That suggests some dissatisfaction with my life. Yet, overriding that dissatisfaction, I watch my self-esteem slowly grow. There, before my peer group, I feel its thriving presence, exhibiting a part of me, in what I do, how I conduct myself, how I approach my existence.

He hesitated for a moment.

Through it all, I must be worthwhile, through it all, my humility must lead me in the right direction. For months I wrestled with the words of the Bible, with the Lord's Prayer, and with the Ten Commandments, but I never heard the music. Now, however, the melody plays across my senses. The chords dance through my thoughts: Melodious chords that peel back the layers of my inner child like an onion. Each of these musical themes is a unique experience. Each has long since become a part of me: A past which unfolds new meanings, and which produces a new symphony and tunes my singing heart.

To approach my essence, the unveiling of a basic love, I require one word: A word which transcends my every day. That word is humility. Humility must be a part of my every thought, my every action, and my every motive if I'm to succeed. My Higher Power will accept me no other way.

The judge interrupted the reporter, "Do not catagorize your salvation under the heading of Christianity. There are other respected religions that satisfy salvation."

I'm sorry. I did not mean to leave out any endeavor that contains a moral content. Of course you are right. There are at least four or five major beliefs that should be included. Will you please forgive my error? It was never my intention to exclude one belief over another. In my haste to explain, I got carried away.

An extended silence carried on for an embarrassingly long time before he spoke again.

Humility can and must allow me to remove the boundaries that guard my emotions. Understand, without the sincerity, that humility allows, without that true heartfelt feeling, my growth would quickly stop. I would stall on the road to recovery. I've already been down one wrong ugly road. It's a trail that leads to a chaotic future. It's a well-worn path to destruction, and it's still taking by many who search for reasons for their existence. Should that happen, and well it might, I would require a change in direction. I would require the all saving Grace of my forgiving

God! So in prayer I beseech God for help. On my knees, with head bowed I come to my Maker and ask for his direction. I blindly ask for forgiveness. Now and then I imagine catching a glimpse of some serious Moslems in an act of contrition, bowing their heads before their Supreme Being. It is this kind of thing they are good at, and it is the type of humility that all Christendom should emulate. I hope it is not too hard a pill to swallow, for any believer. Grace comes to all who make the march toward the handiwork of their God.

Thomas Aquinas believed that Nature by itself led the way to belief in God. Realizing how I fit into Nature's plan has helped to put my thoughts into perspective. However, I'm not blind to the sense of whom and what makes my presence acceptable. I believe that's where the problem lies.

Crying out from every corner of the Globe, millions of souls make their plea, asking for acceptance, asking that their needs be met, asking that their prayers be allowed. On that basis, I stand little chance of gaining a hearing. Is a 'Leap of Faith,' the only avenue I can take? Lip service will not do. There has to be more. Not only should my mind acknowledge and revere my God, but a feeling should sweep through the marrow of my bones, lodge itself in my viscera, and well up in my heart. If I'm, considering just a partial commitment. If by dallying over some ill fated religious point dooms me to failure, God's bridge will never be lower for me to cross. So, I come forward to accept the only way to accomplish the goal of serenity: a belief in my Higher Power. The other way, the way of co-dependency, is not one I wish to choose. That way is more difficult. It is an addiction, and that leads to Sin. It requires a trip down a long and arduous path, down and through the river of fire. I have no stomach for that. Searing my body with the blaze of Hell would, I'm sure, bring me to my senses, and perhaps at a more timely pace. For me, it would be the last resort, and yet, some how I choose that route. It is this transgression, this co-dependency that stains the cloth of my recovery. It is this ever torturous transgression that leaves me scarred. It is where the Ego begins, where a 'Life of Feeling' becomes paramount, where the thrill of living on the rim of excitation begs for recognition: Exhilarating, yes, grounds for salvation, I don't think so.

So I go my way. Each small amends that I spawn gets pulled through the fine sieve of bodily pain. Inexorably my past gets scoured. Nothing stays behind. Hopefully, passing through the river of fire, leaves me somewhat empty of Sin. Let me explain. Sadness claimed me that day. Melancholy claimed me for a much longer time. I spent hours sobbing, swearing at my circumstance, beating back my fear with anger. The sorrow was unrelenting.

I screamed in the shower, where no one could hear me. I pounded on a pillow with a baseball bat until the sweat gushed from my pores. I bellowed, "God, You can't do this. I don't deserve it."

In church I sang the songs of my youth. I knew that most everyone watched the tears roll down my cheeks. I grew ashamed. Steadily, for a year, I endured my fellow pew members. Only the strength of my mother's upbringing kept me coming back.

A worried minister called my home, and arranged for a private meeting. He was willing to listen. That day, in a display of love, he blessed me and put his arms around my chest and hugged me.

This was the turning point, the end of my descent into the river of fire. At that moment I was at the 'nadir' of vanity. Suddenly, the Lord began to show me a pathway out. Feelings of anger, rage, and revenge left me. My ego no longer fought to get even. I began to see my past as neither good nor bad, but only as a necessary part of my spiritual education. Devoid of emotion, I came away, lightheaded and introspectively free. God's bridge was being lower. God began making time for ordinary unheralded me. Looking back, my pathway is clearly visible. At that moment, it felt like I was taking ungainly steps toward a quagmire of doubt. Yet something drove me on. Inadvertently I had found the springboard: A foundation from which to launch my forays into a new spiritual existence. Yes, God had started my motor.

A succession of warm, caring, devout friends entered my life in an implausible way. Had I wanted to list those people, and so to meet them, or someone like them, a dozen years would have slipped by. My quick choices were not accidents. They were orchestrated. I'm sure that God arranged the availability of each acquittance. I had to open my eyes. The word humility remained the key.

How do I keep from becoming vain after spiritual success comes my way? Easy, no—I'm aware what my struggle will always be: Exposure to that part of life demands that I avoid temptations of vanity. Yet, affectations racked me. 'I did this. I did that.'

Anyone, who wants to hear about my successes has only to stop and chat. I'll respond as if it were a Mexican Hat Dance, I, I, I, I.

My dear mother taught me the proper social attitudes. I should know how to make friends, yet my mind resists. Not by direct will power, but unconsciously I fight to get recognition and acceptance from my peer group, perhaps even at the expense of lasting friendships. So, at the end of the day, I scramble home, embarrassed and ashamed, though I know the interlude was not a conscious part of my other self.

I know where I'm heading, but I'll never know how I'm to get there. It's a curse of long standing, second nature for the likes of me. I can't blame my parents, or my environment. I put the blame squarely where it belongs...on me. Yes, God's in his heaven, all's right with the world. Whatever is, is right. I'm here, exactly where I should be at this point in time.

Each step I take signals a lesson learned. So, I must always remember: 'Nothing, absolutely nothing happens in God's world by mistake.'

Energies, once used for flights of fantasy, now charge my spirit and build strength toward reality: a strength that drives me forward on my path to serenity. My co-dependency waddles behind: the behavioral chain is broken. I'm able to operate in the clean air of adult demeanor.

I can never go back to those grotesque days of feelings sorry for myself, of hating those individuals I needed to blame. Now weaned, I find a feeling of satisfaction flooding over me. It's about a future all too wonderful,

Not being perfect, there are times when I feel as though I'm beginning all over again. However, I do not fear failure. I've already come through the realm of total darkness. Prayer, meditation, and honest efforts are my stepping stones to faith. To that end, being truly humble carries me forward.

Straddling a firm foundation, which God showed me how to build, has given me renewed strength. I know my bliss. I have love. I'm a happy man. With gratitude I say, I love my God, and for no other reason.

In closing, all that I say is true. I'll say it again, "Nothing, absolutely nothing happens in God's world by mistake."

I pulled back from my proselytizing. I strengthen my grip on the things I have learned, not only about myself, but about the Good Book, the Bible. I have become a dependable person, willing to show my hand and willing to listen to the words of the Lord.

* * *

The judge reached for a new Kleenex. He wiped the perspiration from his brow. He felt content for the first time in years. Hearing the confession, restored a good feeling in his heart. There was certainly a bit of nobleness in what had been said.

Sister Sarah added a comment, "Things will turn out for the best. Prayer always sets things right. That's why we champion right. Tonight when all of us go to bed, we should have that positive attitude. It will make all the difference in the lives."

A tearful mother, in the audience, spoke up, "I'm not sure I have the strength or the will to do what you ask. Although I'm a believer, it seems as if it's not enough."

"Trust me. It will be more than enough."

"I know you're right and I know you mean well, but my faith is not that strong. I will say this, I'll try to do as you say. If I fail, all I can do is beg forgiveness from my Lord."

Sister Sarah added a sentence, "The Grace that comes from on high will bind our wounds and help us through the days of suffering. Of all the things I've been able to learn, that is the most important."

Another sorrowful mother resting on a chair next to the window spoke of her feelings, "I'm quite sure St. Mary's has done all they can to make future births more secure. Why hospitals have to wait until something dreadful happens like this makes me sick. We pay our money to those establishments for good medical practices, but we also want safety while staying at the hospital. Next time, my family or I need medical attention, the question of where, will not be consideration. St. Mary's is a good place to have medical work performed. Every doctor they employ has an excellent reputation."

She took a deep breath.

"I want to remind you. We're not just talking about doctors. We're talking about safety. I don't believe anyone can find a fault with my position. Worrying about health is bad enough, but worrying about safety should not be a factor. I bring up the problem of bad water. Are you familiar with another hospital where the water turned bad? I'm sorry. Bad water in a hospital is not very sanitary, and it's not being safe. Drinking bad water gives me a scary feeling. Do you know what St. Mary's is going to do about the threat?"

"I'm sure they have implemented the necessary safeguards. They certainly got after that problem right away. As a matter a fact, the board had the plumbers and the micro biologists working well into the night. I've heard no more. They must have the problem in hand. Funny, one of the largest hospitals in Tucson had a similar problem two or three years ago. They had to bring in a fresh water supply. Once they had solved that issue, they were able to dismantle the water lines and inject a chemical solution into the system. It was only a matter of time until they received a clean bill of health."

"Tell me, how long did it take the hospital to fully restore the watering system?"

"Honestly, I'd say about three years. The bug that was in their water was very toxic. I recall it was the germ that breeds Strep infection."

"I don't think St. Mary's water problem is that bad. I believe sone one said it would be cleared up in a matter of days."

Margaret stared off into the night. The ability to place her views into what had happened only registered vaguely. Some of her horrific thoughts remained. Thoroughly scrambled, Margaret's senses reeled off a whole series of ugly reflections. Her face flushed red. She triggered a whine showing her displeasure. Margaret was on the verge of a nervous breakdown. The woman turned to her husband and began an even louder whimper. Longingly she looked to him for strength. It was not to be. Not today, nor would she feel any new strength from Martin in the future. He was too consumed by his own horror.

"What idiot would do a thing like this? I not sure DNA tests will guarantee the identification of our baby. It's a fairly new science, one that the biologists are still trying to work out the kinks. I'd like to believe that the identifications they decide on would be quite positive, but the thought of a mistake? Well, that would shatter my trust in the medical profession."

Breaking the barrier of sanity, his wife announced her train of thought, "Martin, I don't see how a doctor can help me overcome this feeling, but may be that's our only choice."

Her husband paled. The thought of what his wife had just said drove a spike into his lucidity. His senses simply jammed on the brakes.

Margaret continued, "Trusting the lab technicians to analyze and correct the mixup is a feeble hope, but it may be the only hope we have. I've talked to some of the other mothers and they are as uneasy as we are. What the doctor proposes won't do it for me. I'll never be positive that the baby we finally get is ours."

"Sweetheart, we have to believe in something. One thing for sure, our baby is a Caucasian. That may rule out half the children in the nursery. That at least narrows the odds a bit."

"I thought that the nursery had only Irish babies, and those babies were from our group."

"Gosh I never thought of that. I believe you're right. That gives us a better chance to get the right child back."

"I'm going to have the women get together and see if any one of them can positively identify their baby. Some children may have had birthmarks or some small physical difference. Hair color for one, and how much hair could be another. You know what I mean. Of course this must be done quickly, otherwise, those variations will disappear."

Some of the children may easily be identified while others might be the life like images of the child in the next basinet. I'm sure the Mother Superior is aware that the advantage will be ours for only a short time.

"Margaret, wasn't our baby the biggest? Didn't he weigh more than the others?"

"Yes he was the heaviest, but that could change in just a few days. The problem was we found no distinguishing marks."

Martin uttered a sigh, "Can't life be a little easier. We were just starting a family and now this. Six babies in a nursery, and no one knows which parents they belong to. I have to say, what a rotten piece of luck. I had thought that newly married people received a grace period before they were forced to wash back and forth in the breeze like so much flotsam."

"It's more than bad luck. Someone or something has an ugly mean streak running through them. I'd like to believe that of the six families some person might have wanted revenge, but to take it out on all six families is out of line. I've told you that most of my life has been spent in sorrow. When my father died I became aware of a bitterness which made my heart ache. I was just nine years old, but I was not too young to appreciate my parents. When my father passed on, the pain of him leaving left my family scared and lonely. My sense of life became dormant. For the longest time I had no feelings at all. I couldn't figure out why some bloodlines was spared and others were torn asunder. Even my mother, wise as she was beyond her years, had trouble understanding."

"Martin looked at his tear-laden wife and said, "Say, I believe we have a few minutes. I like to relate a story, a true story. Maybe it's not the right time, but I'm hoping it will give you and insight to the feelings of the other people involved. It's about me growing up, and becoming an adult. For want of a better name I'll call it, 'My Father and a Cat named Boots.'

Margaret felt relief. The tangential approach turned her memory page, away from sorrow. She felt like walking over to her kindly husband and kissing him lovingly on the cheek.

Margaret stood and said, "I believe it might be good medicine for the way I feel. I hope it has some answers to my heart aches. The hospital has said nothing, so far, that takes away the pain."

"If you don't like what you hear, I'll stop it, in a minute."

"Martin, is this the time for a story about your past. I don't believe I can concentrate on a boyhood tale."

"Try it for a few minutes. I'm sure the story will entertain you."

"If you're right, go ahead. It will at least be a distraction to me."

"That's rue. Tell me if you can't stand it, and I'll shut it off."

"No. No, I'll promise to listen to the entire tape."

"Well here goes." He moved to the table and turned on the tape machine. The whir started immediately. Quiet descended. The listeners, especially Martin strove to hear the tape. It was not the best recording. The hiss and the wow made him reluctant to continue playing the tape. The look that came from his wife removed all doubt.

I call this: My Father and A Cat Named Boots.

I had barely turned nine when my father's death branded me with a grief I couldn't shake. For a long time I refused to smile. Abject sorrow pressed me to the limit. At such a young, impressionable age, grieving for my father had brought me to the brink of sorrow. You see. I loved my father. He was a stern parent, but he taught me many things about becoming a man.

His cancer left an angry spot in my breast. Disillusioned and most of all sullen, I yearned for the return of an honored father, and my friend. I felt I was too young to lose a parent. I was too young to bear the heartache that ground away at my vitals. Most of all, I wanted someone to explain why fathers' pass on and leave their offspring, to shift for themselves, trying to overcome the pain of despair.

The only other adult in the house, my mother, was unable, then to offer kind words. Filled with her own grief, she tried hard to block the hole in her soul, but it was beyond her. At night I could hear her weeping.

Long after his death, my feelings stayed locked inside me. Mainly because I thought my world had ended. The man I respected and admired had departed from our home. He was so young. No longer my bosom friend, he lay at the Hillside Cemetery, on the northeast side of Minneapolis.

Dad's last night on earth had demanded a weighty decision from me. Should I go to the nursing home, or should I stay in my bedroom, where from that refuge I could remember him as he was. I found it hard to decide. My mother knew how I felt. Even so, she asked me if I'd care to come along. I shook my head. I had visited my Father two days before. Already emaciated, drawn, with the look of death in his eyes, it was this picture of him I wanted to forget. My mother let my answer stand. She and my sister, Lorraine, went without me. When they returned, I saw the red in their eyes and noted the silence. I think I made the right choice.

It was fall. The weather had chilled. Multi colored leaves had been toppling to the ground for days. My mother unpacked our winter coats and hung them in the closet, ready for use. As night fell, a hint of freezing rain filled the air. Now it matched my outlook on life. A bit of morbid despondency ran the gamut of my thoughts. I looked skyward, and asked the eternal, juvenile question, "Why did my father have to die?"

After almost a week of dreary reflections, bleak recall and a bitterness that ate away at my well being, my mother said, "You can't keep this up. It's not right. Young boys should not grieve, at least not for this long."

I answered the only way I could, "I'm doing the best I can. Mom, a guy has to have a Dad. I had so much to learn from him."

"You'll forget everything he told you in a few weeks."

"Oh no, I remember everything he taught me. He was a good teacher."

She scolded me again, "Raymond, did you hear me. Stop it right now. When Joey comes by this afternoon, don't tell him any lies when he asks you to go to the park."

"I promise I'll go to the park with Joey. They have a new swimming pool. Joey says it's neat. Maybe I'll take along my swimsuit and go for a dip. It's an indoor pool. Joey says it's warm inside. It costs only a nickel. I can afford that. Besides, my allowance is due, right?"

"That's my boy. Now you're talking. The two of you can have a good time in the pool. Afterwards, bring Joey home with you. He eats fresh baked cookies, doesn't he? I just finished making a couple dozen oatmeal cookies." My mother's voice droned on. Much of what she said I never heard.

I was still sobbing when I left the kitchen. I couldn't break the pattern of thought. In desperation I ran to the living room and stretched out on the couch near the bay window. I stationed myself where I always had. It was my habit to welcome my father. From the window I had a vantage point. I could see all the way down to the end of the block. I could see him first.

I began imagining a tall angular man walking down the sidewalk toward the house he called home. If I closed my eyes, it was easy.

Walking, fit his day. We didn't own a car: The ugly depression had doled financial sorrow out to most every family. Fiscal ruin came to many. It forced the majority of families to live from paycheck to paycheck. We had also received our share of bad luck. Had my father been able to afford a vehicle, ownership of a car would never have worked. Gas and oil, and alcohol for the radiator, to keep it from freezing, would have seriously damaged the family budget.

My father was nearly seven feet tall, and he wore a size twenty two shoe. Any car was an effort to get into, but it made no difference to me. He was my hero. I myself, in turn, was a stripling of a lad, impressionable and naive. I was too young to understand that life dealt sorrow to everyone who drew a breath. So, I kept hoping, dreaming of his return. The thought kept growing in my heart. I kept praying for that wee light of hope. Was he gone forever?

With supper over, when I knew no one was watching, I returned to the window. My grief made it impossible to stop the tears: I was good at sharing my emotions with the window pane. The glass had already fogged over because of my breathing, restricting my vision. That's how close I was. The distorted view forced me to raise my elbow and wiped most of the moisture away. Now I could peer out. Half in a daze, my eyes closed for a moment, and a wistful memory sailed by. It had always been a thrill, watching my father walking toward the house. Long purposeful strides graceful and light footed, he had the air of a proud and committed father. That had long since vanished. Then, there was nothing, only the gaunt frame, red-eyed and unsteady with the life leaking out of him.

I knew by heart the path that he took from the Grand-Monroe Street Car, at the end of the block, to our door. Now the path would be empty.

At a quarter past five the sidewalk showed motion. A large, woolly black and white cat padded slowly toward our end of the block. Regal in appearance, he had to tip the scales at 15 pounds.

From where our house stood I had a good look at the animal. Intrigued by the marking on the cat, I scurried out the front door and stood on the porch: We had the only house on the block with a front porch. I leaned over and put my arm on the railing watching the approaching animal. I enjoyed the cat's nimble swagger. I had to guess it was part Angora because of the length of its fur. A blaze of white ran down to the edge of its nose. Along with four white paws the kitty brought a yearning to my breast.

Boots, as we later called him walked straight up the five steps to where I was standing. As cats will do, he circled my leg two or three times, rubbing harder against me each time. He finally arched his back on the last loop, stopped in front of me and raised his head and made eye contact. His usual low throaty meow, followed by the cat laying full length on the porch, gave me the feeling that I was acceptable. In a moment he rolled to his back, raising all four paws in the air. I suspect he was asking me to admire his white boots by using a playful gesture. In those first few introductory moments, he had artfully succeeded in making a life long friend.

I knelt down on the porch floor and picked up the cat. I was unable to identify this new emotion, but I did feel a warming sensation flow through my body. Even the idea of ownership danced across my mind. Yes, I conjured up the obvious question.

Would mom let us keep the cat?

I knew my sister liked furry things. A coat and a stole were furry things. I figured a cat was furry. I couldn't see much difference. With some anxiety, I lugged him inside the house. Im made straight for the kitchen and put him on the floor.

I pleaded with my mother, "Please, can we keep the Kitty Cat? See. It doesn't have a collar."

I picked up the black and white Angora and centered myself in the kitchen. I started to whine and connive. I even said I would do the supper dishes, if Lorraine would wipe them.

"Not now my son," she said. "Wait until your sister gets home." My mother gazed at me sternly, "Listen. You remember the enjoyable friendly dog we had. Remember how badly you felt when that car ran over him. Both you and your sister cried the whole day. Do you remember how long it took for the hurt to go away? Further more, I don't think you realize what a chore it is to keep an animal."

"Ah, mom, we'll take care of the cat. Say, may I give him a saucer of milk. He might be hungry."

My mother nodded and decided to reserve judgement till the whole family was present. Much later, my sister got involved. She demanded payment for her yes vote. After being paid a dollar by me, she okayed the feline. Boots became part of the family.

I put the cat on the floor. Out of the corner of my eye I watched him approach my mother. He did the same thing to her that he had done to me. He rubbed against her leg and purred. My mother wiped her hands on the apron tied around her waist and bent down. She stroked the cat once or twice and smiled.

"Well, I don't think your sister will really mind. Being so fluffy makes the cat attractive. I do believe you're right. It must be part Angora." My mother deftly lifted the cat's tail. Determining that it was male, she added, "If he stays around, we'll see. Son, you know he could belong to someone."

Realizing what my mother had said, I still felt Boots sensed I was lonely. Somehow it seemed as if he knew that my best friend had died. The cat seemed to be asking a question. Could this Tomcat become my needed replacement? Could the cat overcome the void my father left?

It dawned on me later. Around the dining room table, after

the cat had turned into a household fixture, it became readily apparent. The cat, Boots, was just what the family needed to take our minds off our father.

My mother, raised on a farm, retained a good grasp of the nature of animals. Training cats was well within her expertise. In a matter of days, Boots responded. In time he learned many tricks on his own. Those antics were thrilling to watch, and often they came off, down right-funny. Rattling the pantry door knob, when he felt hungry was a first in his repertoire. It was immensely popular with my sister and me. We laughed every time because when he had rattled the door nob, he would drop down on all fours and look at us. I venture to say, he believed we were not answering his needs. In the same learning cycle the next bit of cat-intelligence involved his toilet training. My mother had watched him closely that first day. When she saw him, sneak off to a corner of the kitchen, she knew what he was up to. Right after he finished, she grabbed him by the scruff of the neck and stuck his nose in the pile of dung. Still holding on, she deposited the cat outside on the ground. Boots never forgot. I guess, he figured this was an accepted rule in the house. Rattling the pantry door had offered a solution to being fed, so maybe rattling the outside door would offer a solution to the other law of the house. Sure enough, it worked. Now, not only did he use that action to gain entrance, but it worked the same way when he wanted to go outdoors on the prowl.

My mother, pleased with his progress declared, "We'll allow the cat to stay." Boots had evidently measured up to my mother's strict standards. Not wishing to press any advantage, I nodded my head in agreement.

Some time earlier, I had thought about Boots sleeping in bed with me, but now was not the time to ask for that favor. I had learned to ask for only one thing at a time.

Kneeling on the floor, I put my arm around Boots and squeezed him ever so slightly, saying, "Now, you can be my life long friend." With another breath, I said, "Thanks Mom."

Silently, but without hesitation I raised my face toward the sky and repeated my feelings, "Thank you, thanks for my new friend."

The feline association continued for a little over a year. It was Saturday. Boots, now fully grown, had blossomed into a splendid animal. On that weekend morning, I had dawdled. My mother needed to force me out of bed. Leaving the warm covers behind was a chore. It was cold outside, and the thought of shivering until I got dressed made me even more uncomfortable. I had played with Boots and a ball of string until after my bedtime, so getting up was a drag. It lasted most of the morning.

My mother was sharp with her retort, "Son. Do you want a spanking? Do as I say, get out of bed, now!" Worried about my mother's order, I dressed in a hurry. Once clothed, I straightened the covers on the dual-fold sleeper. Folding the bed twice went hard. I had to push down rigorously to close the two parts. Evidently I had not smoothed the covers very well.

About noon the family wondered where Boots was. We had not seen the cat that morning. We had never known him to pass up a meal, so we searched the house.

Boots always slept indoors and under my bed. It was cooler there. Starting the search there by my bed sounded right. When I found Boots under the dual-fold, I let out a yell. I knew what the outcome was. After the bed was closed, the space under it lacked enough clearance for the animal. A spring supporting the mattress lay across his neck. My mother also realized what had happened. She scurried into the room and put her arms around me. Together we cried. Even my sister joined in.

For burial, a large, macaroni box fit Boots perfectly. My sister made a small, black, wooden cross. She tied it with a yellow ribbon and placed it inside. Neither one of us figured Boots would be roasting in Hell, but then you never know. That finished the ritual. We carried the box outside.

At the far corner of the backyard, my sister and I buried our furry friend under a Green Ash tree which was beginning to offer shade. After the burial, I realized that twice, in two years, I had lost good friends: My father and now Boots. As I had done the night my father died, I bucked up and refused to cry.

My mother offered an oath, "Children, this will be the last animal to occupy a place in our house."

She concluded by saying, "Our family luck, with cats and dogs, is undeniably bad."

At my age, my mother's statement was sheer devastation. Again, I had to hold back the tears.

So, I asked her the first question, "Why are pain and suffering mixed in with our freedoms?"

I remembered, it seemed like an experience from the dark side.

My Mother spoke to me in sympathy, "Son, pain and suffering visit most families. I'm sorry to say it happens quite often. Few go unscathed. It's hateful and it weakens the social fabric of the family. In an unstable moment many of us throw out the idea of belief in a kindly Supreme Being. Much of our suffering happens because we lack a view of life's lessons. It shouldn't be that way. Everyone should be aware of the important mile posts in their lives. Education should provide those guidelines regardless of the thought processes that swirl around in schools of higher learning. Any college or university which does not prescribe Science, Literature and the Arts as a necessary part of any degree, are cheating their students out of some thought-provoking experiences. It's also time to add a note of guarded pessimism. Stringent care should be given to the privilege of mentally influencing large groups of people. The public should always insist on some regulation concerning free speech. One may, in private, or in a dialogue say whatever crosses their mind, but when addressing a crowd certain liberties must be withheld. Unless the speaker is a well-recognized expert on the subject matter, he or she should be held responsible for the content. That is one area where the ACLU should take a stand. I might add that even the ACLU falls into the trap of making public statements involving social subjects they are ill advised about. The Constitution reminds us that the most important duty of that parchment is to promote the general well fare. It would serve our government immeasurably well to tune into the majority opinion concerning the subject at hand."

My mother had the last word, "In our need to develop healthy, educational platforms, from which to practice morality, we generally miss, or cover up the happenings of consequence in our young lives. Don't let that happen. Grow older and grow wiser before you let a part of an unrewarding life get you down. Oh, there are moments when the bugles of truth blows hard, but they are few and far between."

* * *

I keep looking for a man like my father. I keep looking for a philosopher king, a man, able to see the duties that are deemed official in government offices, such as the Secretary of State, a statesman who would handle them in princely fashion, a leader, who would be able to guide the fortunes of a country in the right direction, a mentor chiefly looking after his subjects. One willing to make the hard choices, and one willing to look their constituency in the eye of truth, one who does not give way to political pressures.

But many times infallibility does give way to the tedious strain.

It starts with those we deal with on a daily basis. Try as a mentor might, the honesty he possesses is not that strong. Standing on the top of the hill while the lackeys and their employers advance, demands a man of great depth. At that moment the whole of society seems to be against everything the leader believes in. So, try as he might, to be the authentic voice which enhances the moment of truthfulness, he falls short. Every voter knows what should be done, but the idea of financial gain in some disproportionate manner attracts the vipers to the honeycomb.

* * *

It had been four days since the ransom note was left at the hospital. Each family directly involved had read the demands. Several mothers wanted to pay the ransom immediately, but Martin wanted to find a better way to solve the problem.

"Let's not be hasty in our approach to the problem. I want to warn you. We cannot afford to make a wrong decision."

Mostly the men wanted revenge for what had happened. The police agreed. Some fitting, legal, punishment had to be administered. Letting the miscreant, escape the hand of the law would only create more problems in the future.

Margaret spoke to the assembly, "Criminals have a way of repeating successful ventures. The care with which we handle this will stand us in a good stead."

Sheldon advanced another notion.

His voice telegraphed the hatred he held for their tormenter. "I say we stand pat and help the police all we can. Can any of you think of someone that may have had it in for you, or your family? I mean, someone who wanted to get even."

"I've been trying to place some male that's had access to the hospital on a daily basis. So far I've come up with a big fat goose egg. How about you, Joyce, got any ideas?"

"Well, as most of you know I spent part of last summer here at St. Mary's recuperating from an intestinal infection. I did see a lot of people come and go during that time period, but I can't say there are actions which stand out in my mind as suspicious. I can't believe that any of the people I saw would do an ugly thing like that."

CHAPTER IX

Silence held the group. Not one person could think of an enemy who would do such a thing: this thing that was so terribly wrong.

In madding anger the decisions arrived at by family members were all too familiar. The men were generally ready to fight. The women just wanted to get their 'right' child back. Identifying their offspring would be important, but apparently all they could do would be to wait. Each woman felt intense, down trodden despair. That experience drove deep into their psychic. No amount of comfort, by their husbands or relatives could drive away the remorse.

One woman said, "If they cannot properly identify the babies, I'm afraid I'll become suicidal. From the time I was a teenager, I wanted to have a love child of my own. Now I can never be sure that the tot I raise is really my husband's and mine. I have to say this, I've been in a sorrowful mood ever since I found out. My husband tried to ward off my fright, but even his platitudes did no good. Until I'm sure there is no mistake, I will live in fear."

* * *

Across town, the second ransom note was ready to mail. Licking the flap of the envelope, Jeffery Singline folded the flap over and pressed it shut. Next, he placed the letter in a brown paper bag. Then he took off his cotton gloves.

"This ought to get some quick action."

His mind played across the proceeding.

The hospital doesn't know it, but it owes me. Collecting is going to be the crowning glory. It's the right time. I'm going to hound them until I get the money. I've worded the second ransom note stronger than the first. That should bring some attention.

CHAPTER X

"So now, the ball is in their court. I'm not going to move one inch from my position. Considering what they did to me I think I'm entitled. I'm being as fair as possible. Had they listened to me, it could have been different. None of this would have happened."

In thought, his mind hurtled on. He had replayed the dismissal scene many times over the last six weeks. It appeared as though he could think of nothing else. Even his brother felt the compulsion. Toady had told him often enough that his blatant emotions were unfounded, but still he persisted.

Jeffery tarried over the decision. His mind set stayed with the ransom note.

What I'm asking for is well within reason. They've had two days and haven't said yes or no. I want this second note to get some action. I don't want to be tied down for more than two more days. I suppose they're looking at DNA as a way to get around my demands. So be it. That field of science is new. I wouldn't trust the outcome in identifying my child. Hmm, I'd better get moving if this is to go in tonight's mail.

Aloud he said, "If I get no response, I'll call the hospital. It may not be the thing to do, but I use a public phone. If they can't trace the connection, I'll be in the clear."

They might attempt to trace the call. If they do, they'll know they are not dealing with some knuckle head. But calling them could give them the impression that I'm in a panic. That is not good.

Hum, slow down. You're in a good position. You just have to wait. Give them the time they need. Assert yourself only when you have to. They know, and you know that time is on your side.

Jeffery turned to look at his face in the mirror. He was hoping to see a calm deliberate visage. Instead he saw a confused look. Deep lines hugged his cheeks. Darkening circles rested under his tired eyes. His skin had a cold, clammy look. There were signs that his limbs were shaking slightly. Moving closer to the mirror, he peered at the reflection. The look told of the absence of sleep. His breathing was unsteady, and he had a suspicious rasp in his voice. To say that he was on the winning side might have been stretching the truth. One thing he knew, he had to do was call his brother. It had been days since they talked. Conversations with his older brother were always reassuring.

* * *

Toady lived in the southern part of England. It was a small agricultural town about forty miles from London. Toady, as an older brother knew what Jeffery was up to. He wanted no part of the scheme, but Jeffery had dragged him into the conversation at the outset. As a result, he had become a sounding board for Jeffery. From its inception he had been privy to the entire scheme.

At the very beginning Toady announced his dislike.

"Jeffery, what you are doing is a calloused misdeed. No good will come of it. This action will settle in your heart and make you sorrowful for the rest of your days."

For Toady, to be involved was the last thing he wanted to have happened, but blood proved to be thicker than water. He knew he couldn't turn down his younger brother. Family didn't do that. To have said no to the incident would have been to douse the family values in a bath of ice cold water.

So Toady kept up the pretense, nodding his head even though he knew action was wrong.

Another day came and went. In the hospital, the police were everywhere. Jeffery knew that getting into St. Mary's would be difficult. Still, he had promised to straighten out the mess after St. Mary's paid the ransom. The young ex-doctor was not a mean man. He however, did need the money.

Leaving the name tags as they were originally placed on the cribs was his intention. The ransom note stated he would return each baby to its correct position. That secret was tucked safely in his wallet. He had given the hospital specific instructions. The note stated it would require less than ten minutes to return the infants to their original beds. The ransom note had emphasized the need to leave each bed as it was. Each eight-hour shift was given the same instructions. (Make sure that no one comes in the nursery and attempts to change the position of the cribs.) The orders are clear. The future of St. Mary's is in the balance.

When the nurse found out what had happened she made sure that the cribs remained exactly where they had been. She issued the orders that acted as a safeguard. Night shift janitors were introduced to the ransom note. After reading the demands, they were very aware of the part they were to play. Each worker assigned to the nursery floor realized the gravity of the situation. The conversation always wound up with the same question: How does the marauder expect to infiltrate the hospital guard?

Unfortunately, the place where Jeffery had entered now had several uniformed officers patrolling that part of the building. There was little chance he could slip by without being noticed.

He shook his head and said, "There has to be a way. Perhaps some uniform would help my cause, but what would it be."

Then it struck him, the uniform of Ronald McDonald, "It would not surprise anyone to see that uniform inside the hospital area. The clown appeared quite often at the hospital to entertain the children undergoing hospital care."

He added more to the monologue. "It might even get to the point where I could catch the officers off guard."

CHAPTER XI

His brother, Toady, had dressed for the part two years before, to be exact. He had been part of a promotion to improve the sales of McDonald's hamburgers. His success had given him a day to remember.

Jeffery began to think.

Toady must know where the uniform is. I can phone and ask. I'm sure he can tell me the location of the Ronald McDonald garb.

In early afternoon the call came to his brother.

"Hello," Toady said.

"Hey, remember me. It's Jeffery. I wanted to ask you about your old costume. You know the one: It was a copy of the Ronald Mc Donald costume that we saw on T.V. I need to borrow it to finish my business at St. Mary's Hospital."

Toady knowingly offered, "Well, you can go over to the old house where we lived. Maybe you can find it."

"Did you put it in the back or front of the shed?"

"I believe it's in the front. You need to look in a brown box with red writing on the side. I hope you can find it before it gets dark."

"I know you shoved it into the utility shed, and I know it has

171

not been worn since. Tell me, is it close to the door of the shed so I can get at it? Damn, I wish you were here."

"Hold on, what's the hurry? You know I can't come home at a moment's notice. It would take a week for me to fly back to the States. You just have to pull open a few boxes, and look"

"Save the yackking, will you. You don't have to be here. I'll just knock on the back door and let myself in. I still have a key to the place."

"Didn't the neighbors, down the block, buy the place? I know you gave me my share of the sale."

"I didn't come clean about that," Jeffery said.

"That deal fell apart. I know to have asked you to return the money would have hurt like the dickens, so I didn't say a word. That was the year you wanted to go back for your doctorate. I would have been a chump to ask you to return the money. It would have screwed up all your plans."

"Jeffery, you don't have to be my nursemaid. I'm a big boy. If the deal had fallen through, I could have raised the cash. In retrospect I think my part of the payoff sat in the bank for over a year. I would have just given you back the money."

"I see no reason for crying over spilled milk. The house is worth a lot more now. Which means, I'll come out way ahead of the game. Anyway I like the old place. It brings back good memories."

"Suit yourself. I'm happy to leave the bargain just the way it is. You treated me fairly, and I won't forget that. Deep down, you're a fairly decent guy."

Jeffery spoke quickly, "Toady, this is what I think. With that uniform on, I can sneak past the guards. They'll never suspect Ronald McDonald of any foul play. You know some people are above suspicion, and I believe this character, Ronald McDonald is above suspicion. He's so far removed from the truth of what is happening at St. Mary's that no one will suspect."

"I don't want to know about your scheme. The less I know, the better off I'll be. Jeffery, you never asked me about your little ploy. So why have you involved me? You know, if you get caught it will go hard with you, and it will go hard with me. If my employer finds that out, I'll be out of a job. It's something I'd frown at."

He heaved a sigh and continued his prognosis.

"They will throw the book at you. Damn, if they catch you, you'll never see me again. For both our sakes I'll vanish. If they hook you, a jail is one place I don't wish to visit. As I said before, my employer won't put up with any brushes with the law. I like my job. I was lucky to be in the right place at the right time. The human resource manager goes to my church. That's how I got this chance. It was the big break I had hoped for. Working at Farley Electronics on the east side of London is what I dreamed about for a long time. They treat me just swell. I've always wanted to work there, but if I screw up and get in some serious trouble they'll kick me out. So, if you get caught for what you did, and for that matter, what more you intend to do, I won't have a job. It would be easy for them to find out about our relationship. Being related to you will get me the boot. I would never forgive you for me being turned away from the only employment I ever wanted."

Jeffery yelled at his brother, "Knock it off will you. You never turned down any extras that came your way before. I intend to be careful. Be sure of one thing. I won't squeal."

Toady made a circle of his living room. The phone connection was starting to break up.

"You know. It's my rear end too."

Toady passed a sentence back to Jeffery, "I don't feel like spending the rest of my life in a jail cell. If it were next to my brother, I'd soon learn to despise him."

Then Toady snickered aloud.

Jeffery hardly heard his brother's retort, "Yeah, I know. All the crooks say that. That's why the prisons are crowded. You don't have a lock on being a brain."

"Once upon a time you were a fine doctor. When they caught you sniffing the white powder, they pulled your licence. Now you're just another bum on the street trying to make a score. I can't understand why you would ever do such a foolish thing. To give the medical profession all that time and then lose the chance to cash in. The money you borrowed for your tuition had to be into the six figures. I really feel you did a dumb thing, but it's all over now."

"It was a dumb thing, but when you're young you do dumb things. I'll take what's coming to me, and I won't grumble."

"Well, who knows, the AMA might reinstate you after awhile."

"I doubt it very much. This doctor, one of the board members, never liked me. He's the one who cast the tie breaking vote. He will never change his mind. Forget about my guilt. I never said I was innocent. It's my cross to bear. There are some things you do not know. If you did know, you'd have a better grasp of the picture. Anyway, I'm not crying over spilt milk. One thing for sure, I will never ask you to go to the wall for me, but I do expect you to pass on any ideas that cross your mind, okay."

"That's an attitude I can live with. Listen, brother. I hope you hit a home rum, but don't expect me to chase all your foul balls. I've got too much to lose."

Jeffery's voice spoke offensively, "Go ahead and talk like a smart ass. Lucky you're a relative, or I kick your rear end."

"I wouldn't try that if I were you. I swing a mean set of dukes as you well know. The last time you got smart with me, you landed in the hospital. Listen, the cooperation you get from me is the best I have to offer. You're fortunate. I could report you to the police."

"Ah, sure, and cows give chocolate milk."

Jeffery's call waiting alarm rang. He stopped his conversation with Toady long enough to say "Hello."

Hitting the hold button Jeffery said, "St. Mary's is on the line. Their legal department is calling to tell me there are some papers I needed to fill out. Why should I do that for the hospital?"

"If you want reinstatement, you do what the department wants." His brother's clipped sentence did not go unnoticed, but it ended the call. Was the hospital insinuating they might drop all the drug charges and give him another chance? Jeffery's heart took an extra large beat. What saliva he had in his open mouth dried up. Sweat crept onto his forehead. The thought of what he was hearing tore at his feelings. He had evidently made a huge mistake. Being sorry did not fit the bill. He would have to do more to repair the damage, but now was not the time.

Jeffery said the words, "I think I've been bitten by a snake. Every day this problem gets worse, but no matter what comes-down, I can't lose my brother. I know he wishes this had never happened, and I guess I feel the same way, but the mess is on the table and a clean rag won't wipe away the stain. Maybe when this is all over, we can get back to basics. Having a beer at the local tavern can heal a good many wounds. Crap. I don't know how to get out of this jam. To go to the hospital and admit I'm the perpetrator of the switch at the new born nursery means I'll go to jail. Even though I can solve the identification problem, who's going to care. Either way, I'm in a bind. I should call my brother back and ask him what to do."

Jeffery dropped onto the bed and began to examine all his options. Sleep interrupted his thoughts. He never stirred from that position. Sleeping, uncovered the entire night, left a chill in his muscles.

The dream that unfolded in his mind had some basis in fact. He had always been interested in airplanes. His brother had even wanted to fly. Now, it appeared as if he might. Virtual realism ran rampant through Jeffery's thoughts. Each physical attribute stormed across his mental processes as though it were real. Straining mightily to remember all the nuances, Jeffery discovered that the adventure was not about him, but it was about his brother.

The intensity of his thoughts pushed forward. Realism grabbed the stage front and center. The deep concentration forced a picture to appear as though it were virtual certainty.

The dream came to him in first person dialogue.

The mental video began, "I'm rattled. Damn, this cross country flight has actually made me frightened."

His thoughts raced on ahead. "Maybe a sexual romp between the sheets would help. Susan could come over. That would calm my nerves. What was her last name anyway? Wait a minute, Kagan, that's it." Toady Singline punched in the number. On the second ring, Susan lifted the phone, and listened to Toady's petition.

"Sure…I'll come by about seven. You'll need time to shower."

"Fine," Toady answered.

At seven the doorbell rang. "Come in," He yelled. "Hey, do you wanna a beer?"

"I'd rather have a glass of wine."

"Sorry, beer is all I have."

"That's fine. Sure, I'd like that."

Toady pulled at the door on the refrigerator. He grabbed two bottles of cold beer and walked over to the settee. Settling in beside her, he placed the bottles on the table. The beer tasted good, and a ribald joke or two, swung their mood steadily toward sensuality. Offering a seemingly affectionate hug and kiss, Toady took command. The experience, though not totally physical, rode deep into his body. Susan, aware he had enjoyed himself, smiled. When it was over, he put a hand on her shoulder, patted her and rolled to a sitting position. For a moment he pondered the evening. She wondered too.

"You were hot stuff," He said.

"Did I do something special?"

"No, but it was good. I really enjoyed myself. Sorry about my attitude. I'm worried. It's the scary, cross-country flight I'm taking Thursday. I'm actually squeamish about going. I called you because I thought sleeping with you would settle my nerves."

She never heard the next sentence. Right then, she knew she had figured this guy wrong. He was a jerk. Downcast, Susan stuffed her ponderous girdle into a carry-bag. Bending over, she pulled on her knee-high stockings and slipped into her shoes.

Tactfully she remarked, "Be careful. Flying solo is difficult. Without enough sleep it could be dangerous. Have you thought about that?"

Unimpressed, Toady replied, "Sure, sure."

Miffed by his casual comment and lack of affection, Susan managed a very curt, "Goodbye!" She pulled hard at the door and announced her displeasure by slamming it shut.

That focused his attention, enough to say, "Bye." He added a sentence, "Damn, there's a strange odor about her."

The distraction lasted less than a minute. His thoughts returned to the Cessna aircraft and the trip.

Practicing law permitted Toady to enjoy flying. It was the one avocation he truly found pleasure in. Airplanes were his passion, and soloing a lifelong dream. A year of flight instructions got him his wings. It was late in life, but worth it.

Paul, his instructor had scolded him, "You did well on the written examination, but I'm cautioning you. Make certain the plane you buy has extra space between the rudder pedals. If it doesn't, you'll be in trouble."

"That's true," Toady said, viewing his feet. He blushed.

"Pushing both rudder pedals, at the same time is not a good practice. I remembered the day you told me to remove my shoes. Ha, that's when I finally soloed. It only took about an hour."

Toady turned to leave. His flight instructor saluted the aviator, and said, "Good luck. Keep working on coordinating your feet."

Alone at last, Toady's exhilaration exploded, "I got my ticket—my wings. Friday, I'm going to buy that Cessna. It's the perfect plane."

That weekend, Cal Rodney, the bank's loan officer, handed him a cashier's check, and Toady headed for Taylor Airport to buy the plane.

Sal, his name for the aircraft, had two seats, front and rear. The aluminum skin added to her looks. Topping that, Sal cruised at 110 knots—130 knots at top speed. With 304 cubic inches of engine, the aircraft had "Toady" written all over it.

Mr. Wilkins, the salesman, tallied the aircraft's maintenance history, "The last tuneup occurred in 2002, 100 hours ago. That leaves two years of flying before an overhaul. You're aware the owner updated the electronic gear? The plane is fully equipped and certified for night flying."

"Yes I know. It's one reason I decided on this plane."

Grinning, Toady handed Jim the check. Signing the receipt, Wilkins placed the check in his briefcase.

Walking out the door, Toady reflected whimsically,

"Dreams do come true; I have my plane."

With constant practice, his handling of the ship improved. Sal idiosyncrasies, even without his shoes, took all Toady's skill. He was miffed. His senses kept nagging him to 'Do Better.'

Paul, his instructor had warned him, "Cross-country trips are essential if you want to use your plane for more than airport hopping. Before your cross country flight, have Mooney inspect the plane. He's expensive, but he's a fine A-and-E mechanic. Spend a buck. Be safe."

"Good idea," Toady said.

In the morning, he landed at the airport and taxied toward Mooney's hanger.

Collaring the man, he said "They say you're the best inspection mechanic at Lincoln airport."

Mooney snickered, "I may be the best, but I charge the least. It's a hundred for a thorough job."

"That's reasonable."

Mooney spent three hours examining every bolt. Later, he signed the A-and-E certification of inspection.

"Hey, Singline, your Cessna's in good shape. I'd fly it to Seattle myself."

"Mr. Mooney, I need your advice. I've reviewed procedures. I've practiced landings, spins and powered dives, and I even bought new tires, but I'm still nervous. Does that tell you something?"

"Yeah, sure, you're one scared chicken. Some pilots wait years before a cross country. In the summer time, heat-driven storms are the main reason planes fall out of the sky. Schedule the flight for the first part of the year. Weather, that unforgiving beast, is calmer in the springtime. It's April now. That says you can go anytime."

Toady nodded, "Sounds right to me. Thanks for the tip."

Incoherently grumbling, Mooney took Toady's check in full payment. Raising his hand in a bored, weak salute, he sauntered off toward his dingy office at the rear of his hangar.

Toady turned on the key and started the engine, and taxied his plane over to tie down area, and then drove home.

CHAPTER XII

His cross-country would start in Waco, Texas with one, scheduled refueling. Installing extra tanks would allow Sal to carry 135 gallons of fuel: heavy loading for the plane, but safe. At 8,000 feet, Sal's range would be 2400 miles. He decided to land at Denver for a refueling stop. Toadies knew that landing at Denver gave him a good margin of safety.

The young aviator smiled, "With any luck, I'll be flying over the mile high city's treetops in seven hours."

At Taylor Airfield, piping the auxiliary tanks had turned into a major project. He had two connections left to tighten when Susan walked up to the plane.

"Take me along," she begged. "It would mean a lot."

He muttered incoherently, *Crap, I never shut up. Telling her about my trip was a mistake.* Aloud, he argued, "Susan, the plane's already overweight."

"Aw, come on, you're a good pilot. Carry less gasoline. Then you'll have enough room for me. I've never been to the State of Washington. It'd be fun."

"Let me check the fuel consumption and I'll call you."

Murmuring again, he said, "How did I get into this scrape? It was never my intention."

Waggling his shaggy head, he added, "Where's my common sense. Susan on aboard would be a distraction I don't need. It's ludicrous."

Annoyed by his thoughts, he climbed down from the wing leaving the two brass ferrules…the remaining fuel connections loose in their sockets.

Thursday dawned along with an air of expectation. Apprehensive about the flight, nausea greeted his stomach. Still sleepy as he rounded a turn at the Taylor Airport, Toady scraped a fender on a parking-lot, light standard. That irked him.

Backing into a reserved stall, he hollered, "Easy, calm down, just get your supplies unloaded." Approaching the Cessna, he tossed a duffle-bag aboard. Then, he walked directly to the control-tower.

"My name is Singline. I need clearance for my cross-country flight."

The elderly clerk smiled, "Haven't seen the likes of you before. You're new. Good luck on your trip."

Toady placed his flight-plan in his sleeve pocket and looked at his watch. It read six o'clock.

Enplaning, he turned the ignition key, and listened to the noisy starter. A few puffs of smoke from the exhaust and the Franklin engine's staccato barks snorted across the runway.

Toady looked over the instruments. The readings were correct. He teased the throttle forward. The six cylinders growled. Excessive fuel gradually cleared the combustion chambers, and the engine's rumble settled into a rhythmic roar. Sal rolled slowly toward the north runway. With rudder control, Toady booted the tail around. The tower's, green light blinked. Checking the carburetor heat, he released the brakes and opened the throttle.

The runway gradually changed to a blur. Sal bounced off the ground once and then slipped into a long, steep bank. Glancing at the compass, Toady whistled.

"Cross-hairs are on NNW; that's great. There's Lake Whitney below." In that direction, Sal pulled higher into the clean, Texas air. Behind him, to the left a near bright sun climbed into view. Twisting his visor to the left, Toady blocked the sun's angled glare.

He mused, "Though I'm a bit nervous, I'm sure the following two days will be a fun time."

Predictably, the weather was holding. Edging the plane toward 7,000 feet, he heaved a sigh, trimmed the aircraft, and leaned back. Looking down, he marveled at the flat Texas Plain. The fertile green plains cut into so many geometric shapes amazed him. Acre after acre showed ownership in that way.

Over Raton, New Mexico the weather changed. Toady looked at the horizon, looking anxiously for the purple hued Rockies. Greeting him instead was boiling, grayish green, cloudy skies. Close by, to the north, spears of lightning darted to earth. Thunderclaps trampled across the horizon. Head winds began buffeting Sal, spinning the compass. Sometimes, the wind shoved the plane forward. Sometimes the wind swirled, blowing the plane off its course. Twice the airspeed indicator reached 300 knots. Toady tried to reduce air speed by pulling back on the throttle. He fought the plane for control.

An eerie sensation crept up his spine; was he losing it?

"My next checkpoint is due! Switch on the radio. Now, don't panic; you're a trained pilot." Edging the craft lower, he searched the clouds for an opening. He could see nothing that looked like a patch of blue sky.

"It's no use: I'm hemmed in by the storm pattern."

He arched his stiff back, and let out a yell. Steadily the aircraft pummeled his body. His left side rib cage ached. A bloody gash swelled on his forehead where his head had hit the cabin rim.

"Denver—crap. I'll never find it in this godforsaken weather?" Terrified, he checked his fuel. The tanks show thirty gallons.

"That isn't enough. I'd better switch to the auxiliaries."

Opening the valve, startled him. About twenty gallons trickled in and then nothing.

"There's no fuel in the tanks!" Then he remembered. During his indecision about Susan he had forgotten to tighten the fuel lines.

Cursing, he said, "Damn her, the fuel is gone, and she's to blame. One lousy time in the fart-sack and the woman takes hold like a pit bull. Hell, you'd think I'd promised to marry her."

The radio began belching static. Changing channels proved useless, but he managed to reel off a 'Mayday' message. Hanging the headset over the armrest, he leaned forward to check the air temperature.

"Twenty degrees!" In sympathy, his body reacted. His teeth chattered. The icy cold brought to mind Susan's chilly departure.

That same night, she had telephoned him and confessed, "Toady, I seldom accept evening engagements. When I heard about your trip, I decided to pamper you, maybe talk you into taking me along."

"Come on Susan, forget it. To you, I'm a number. You don't care about me. You just want the excitement. Do you do this often? I mean, pushing men into compromising positions?"

He heard her voice change, "So I've slept with a few men—so what."

Susan was comely with chestnut hair and good skin. With a suntan thrown in, she appeared well preserved for her years. Her appetite for colors bordered on the unusual, but her choice of stylish clothes tastefully displayed a rare talent.

Susan's heft had bothered Toady: A thick waist, banded by a pink girdle daunted his senses. For Toady it was a new experience. One he felt inclined to remember. Watching her, peel-back the corset made him want to laugh. The feminine shape she had, when the corset dropped away, showed her age.

She had peered hard at him when he let out a giggle.

Susan did like to tease. Witty in a vulgar way, with her back and forth bantering, she was often uproariously funny. Toady seemingly enjoyed the stream of epithets and pungent sexual stories parading from her mouth.

His last exclamation was her odor, "I can still smell her, much like the Gulf's coastal fisheries. She wasn't dirty. In fact, her odor was more of an antiseptic smell, a medicinal smell. Huh, one of the reasons, I didn't want to take her along."

Senses whirling, he spoke again, "Odor—smell? Hell, that's it. She works for a cannery. That's the smell of caustic soda. The canneries clean their machinery with that stuff." Slapping the dashboard, Toady grimaced, "I've made a mistake, but I'd be foolish to tell her."

A diving aircraft brought back reality.

"Whoa, I'm spinning: left on the rudder. Bring the nose down, right on the aileron, gain speed. Gosh, talk about turbulence. Flatten it out, steady. Cripes, I feel foolish talking to myself."

At four thousand feet, the Cessna stabilized. The wind slowed. The Franklin engine purred. Instruments began reading normally. His heartbeat eased. Ahead, the outline of the mountains perked his senses.

"Oh, oh" he shouted. "Higher, I've got to take the aircraft higher. At this altitude, I won't clear the mountains."

Dead before him, to the right, a snow, capped peak poked through the clouds.

"Mount Shasta? That's odd. I shouldn't see Shasta for two

more hours? I can't have come this far. I'd be out fuel." He read the fuel gauge.

"I still have twenty gallons. What other mountain is this high? Something's wrong. Something is haywire. And Kogan was right. I'm tired."

Efforts to control the plane had drained him. He wanted to close his eyes. Locking the joystick in a neutral position, he adjusted the trim tab and released his safety belt. Crawling into the rear seat, he laid his head back on the neck support. The throbbing eased.

"There's room to stretch out. I can relax my cramped legs…."

"Hey, don't do this. What if you fall asleep?"

He remembered. Susan had said he would tire.

"She was right on the money."

Yawning, his head drooped. He fought hard, wrestled with the idea, and nodded off.

Twenty thousand counts later, he woke. The color red showed in his left eye. Pain hammered his forehead. A damaged right eye refused to focus. Taking a breath, he tried to wipe away the inky, pink cloud. It didn't work.

"I remember trimming the plane, and getting into the rear seat."

In the gloom of twilight, his good eye searched the cabin, "I've crashed. I can't hear the engine. Damn, it's cold."

A flashlight helped him check his watch. It had been near two when he last looked. Now, the hands pointed to eight.

An undulating motion caught his attention, "What is that coming from?" Inquisitive, his fingers reached out, feeling along the cabin wall toward the door latch.

"Ouch."

His hand found cold metal and he pushed the door handle open. A blasting wind poured through the opening. Instinctively he yanked the door shut.

"What's going on? At five this morning, Seattle's temperature measured sixty degrees. Here, it must be twenty or thirty below."

Hungry and cold, he searched his duffle bag for blankets, a parka, and rations. Finding an oblong, red can, he peeled back the cover, and swallowed two sardines.

"I don't dare shut my eyes. What did Susan say, 'Stay awake?' Hmm, the food helps."

He settled in. He warmed. The blood drained from his head. He fought a moment, then his eyes closed again. For Toady, night came quickly. Hours later, frigid air and a blinding sun probed the plane's interior. His aching legs and bloody head forced his eyes to focus.

He cautioned himself, "Pay attention. Put your sunglasses on; the glare could blind you."

He blinked and sat upright. The landscape grabbed his attention.

Rubbing his good eye in disbelief, he said, "Snow? On the mountain peaks, in the valleys, everywhere it's white. I can't believe this." Then, he noticed Sal.

Wedged in a crevice on an ice flow, shorn of both wings, the aircraft showed no promise of salvage.

Clambering free of the plane, he said, "Am I dreaming? There has to be some mistake."

As the rising sun warmed the frozen land, the crescendo of falling ice penetrated the silence. Huge chunks began peeling off the ice floe. Shading his eyes, a tear dragged down his half-frozen face. At the edge of his chin a small icicle formed. He looked again at the massive, bluish-white glacier ice and cringed. A cough, and a violent wheeze, magnified the quiet. The noise drove harshly toward his frosty ears, gnawing at his fading sanity. He pulled the rabbit fur hood around his head, warming it. Wrapping the eiderdown blanket around his waist helped. Toady glanced around.

Looking at the surrounding he said, "I think its time to pray. I did well to bring the duffel bag. The clothes—the blankets, the hood, they're lifesavers. Without them, I'd be dead meat."

At the ocean's edge, farther down the unrelenting line of high ridges, another white mass sheared free from the cliff. In awe, he stared at the display; part of the glacier plunged into the ocean. A huge water-crown arose. Surfacing, the massive chunk of ice stabilized. Displaced water boiled up around its edges.

Flushed, Toady hollered, "Beware, sailors! This one's dangerous." High-school physics came to mind. "Two-thirds of any iceberg is submerged under water. Good gosh, that's about one quarter of a square mile below the surface."

Now, something broke the silence a hundred yards astern. Turning, Toady peered ahead, caught the scene and smiled. A double pronged tail, great in size, and streaked with white, slapped the frigid water.

"It's a grey whale sounding! Wow. The tail must be forty feet across." Rising again, mouth full of krill, the whale, half the length of a football field floated momentarily on the ice encrusted water. A stream of water raced skyward from its blow hole.

"I hope its gut is full."

Toady belched, his stomach reeled, "Food, I could use some."

Observing the changing landscape, Toady watched the sun's huge, red orb begin to sink into the western sky. In awe, he marveled as the radiant globe cast an eerie, scarlet glow over the landscape.

"Ah, nature…how beautiful."

Toady ate the rest of the sardines. He realized the distress call had not been answered. That disturbed him. It was not the way the system was supposed to work.

Whitecaps began spattering the floe, as twilight brought on heavier winds. Sal giggled a bit, broke away and rolled sideways into the choppy water. Small chunks of blue-white, lumpy pudding poured over the fuselage. Toadies slight body quivered as Sal disappeared. The thought of tomorrow, without food, slammed home.

Head bowed in abject acceptance, he spoke, "Here, you don't die violently. You slowly…."

A week later, the Waco Gazette covered the bizarre story. The headline was written as follows; An Expired cross-country Pilot was found off the southern shore of Alaska. After a search, no sign of an airplane was discovered. Oddly, the man had a silver key in his left hand. He was holding it in a tight vise grip. Perhaps it was the key to his airplane. It's been suggested that no one will ever know the significance of the key.

Susan Kogan read the article with great interest.

She pursed her lips and raised an indecent smile. Remembering the conversation concerning sleep brought her cautioning, into focus.

"I warned the guy, but he brushed off my alarm. I don't know, but it may have saved his life." A second idea arrested her thoughts.

"Had he decided to take me along, I might have been a part of this obituary. Instead I'm here reading about the death of Toady Singline. I guess fate plays a part in everyone's life."

* * *

Jeffery Singline was in a funk. There appeared to be no way he could out on top of this dilemma.

Now more than ever he realized how much his brother had objected to his actions, and how right he was. The question loomed over his head continually. Could he find a way to save himself and correct the damage he had launched in the nursery?

One way or another he knew his skin was on the line. Since his intrusion into the hospital nursery his life had changed markedly, the apt phrase was 'downhill.

Maybe I could find a way into the hospital and fix things. If I could escape unnoticed it would be the ticket to a peaceful end. From now on, you'd better pick a path that keeps you out of trouble. Listening to your older brother might be a good place to a start. Don't discount your brother's thinking. He may be smarter than you realize. You should have considered the fact that he went through school getting straight 'A's on his report card. Even in college his grades were above average.

Jeffery's grades marched to a different drum beat: Getting better grades in school meant very little to him. However, when he decided to become a doctor all that changed. The bug, of curiosity, got the better of him and his appetite for medical information and better grades soared. Now the days for studying were too short. Burning the midnight oil became a regular habit. Going to bed before the sun came up was a rarity. His eating habits consisted of fast foods and coffee. He lost weight, and the pallor of his skin looked anything but healthy. After the third year in Medical school, he developed a tick. The tick made him cough incessantly and in class proved to be a distraction to the rest of the medical students. The Professor asked that Jeffery take his Lab work in another room. The Professor agreed to wear a microphone, and the verbal class work was relayed to Jeffery over a loud speaker in the laboratory across the hall. Two weeks to the day his eyes became infected. His right eye began to constantly drain a clear liquid. Jeffery as a student now became a patient in the hospital where he was studying to be a physician.

He spent twelve days in recovery. Back on a reasonable diet, and getting the proper amount of sleep, his return to health progressed rapidly. A smile played across his face, and a lighthearted feeling poured into the anticipation of the following weeks. There was little need to explain what had happened. Jeffery had allowed his work ethic to push his physical body beyond its endurance. It was a lesson he would use quite often with his patients after he graduated.

The end to his introspection came abruptly. It was a knock on the door gave realism to the center stage. Twisting out of his chair he approached the heavy oak front door. Jeffery peered through the glass prism. What he saw standing on the stoop gave him cause for alarm. Two policemen were standing there, facing the entrance.

"The jigs up," Jeffery intoned. "They know! I'm screwed. Damn, the fats in the fryer. They have caught me with my britches down."

Twisting the knob, the door rode open. Each officer took a step forward. The taller of the two men extended a hand toward Jeffery and addressed the owner, "Good morning Sir. We've come to see you, In the past you have been very kind in your support of the Children's Fund. This year more than ever, additional money is needed to carry forward on the pledges the police department made to the organization I just mentioned. Can you see your way clear to repeat the amount you donated last year?"

An air of silence sliced through the atmosphere. Jeffery inhaled deeply. Again he had jumped to a conclusion not in keeping with the true reason the officers were standing at his front door.

"Ah, well, sure, I think I can treat the program as good as I did last year." In truth Jeffery was searching for the last twenty-dollar bill he owned. One of the officers opened a manila file and drew a line through his name. The other policeman extended his hand and offered a warm handshake. Having accomplished their goal, they both turned and walked down the steps and turned toward their squad-car. With a sigh of relief, Jeffery closed the door and made his way back to the kitchen.

CHAPTER XIII

Turning on the gas burner, Jeffery started his breakfast again, a task he had begun when the door bell rang.

"I think scrambled ham and eggs would be a good choice."

He open the various cabinet doors and pulled at drawers until he had the necessary parts to his breakfast. The skillet was already melting the butter, so he cracked the eggs and spilled the yellow and white interiors into the pan. The smell became an enticing aroma. Day after day, he waited for the smell to rise to his nostrils, there to tease him into hunger. It never failed.

"I often wondered how one person could eat that many eggs and not get tired of the taste." The riddle had been solved some time ago, when he discovered that dry cereal was not the introduction he wanted for his stomach at day's dawning.

"I give thanks for the eggs in the morning, breakfast routine. I don't like dry cereal, and I dislike hot cereal too. Spreading fruit on dry cereal gives my stomach some relief, but not as a steady diet. It is still an effort to choke down dry cereal. Shucks, I can always vary an egg breakfast by adding celery and onions to the pan."

The eggs having been scrambled turned to a nice tan color.

The toast, done to a tee, popped out of the toaster. He slid the eggs and the toast onto a small sized plate. Before sitting down at the table, he buttered the toast. Then he poured a tall glass of milk. Four out of the seven days this food was the bill-of-fare.

Jeffery never complained. For dinner and for lunch he would eat out. He had never been able to find a favorite place to eat. However, his selection of food always included the bizarre.

Often he would meet people in a restaurant quite by accident and strike up a conversation that lasted through the entire meal. These people generally became friends and even came to St. Mary's Hospital for treatment: such was his bedside manner.

* * *

Mother Superior, winnowed away a day and a half without coming any closer to solving the case. All the depositions were in and cataloged. Many of the workers repeated what had been told previously. Nothing new appeared, and that was a bit unsettling.

It was held that what was known about the incursion, for the time being, had befuddled the security group. Sister Sarah, alone in her office racked her thinking cap.

"Who, at the hospital knew enough, or had done a brisk business with St. Mary's, to initiate this dreadful act." She had listed any number of names, but all to no avail. Her thoughts left that group of people. She also finished with a selected, smaller professional group that had contact with the hospital: That led to nothing of interest. The next parcel, but not the last one involved doctors that had left their practice. Insurance rates had skyrocketed. Many doctors opted out of the profession, devoid of the financial ability to pay the insurance premiums. The 300% rise had gotten out of hand, and there was the chance that premiums would keep on increasing. Should that happen the effect would cause many to take down their 'in business' signs. Insurance costs would be the death knells for the practices of many good doctors.

That point by point investigation of the crime had led to a dead end. Down to the last category, Sister Sarah shuddered. There was only one file left, that of a Jeffery Singline. Opening his files, she read extensively.

Aloud she muttered, "Good diagnostic ability. Jeffery had excellent bedside manners. He was well taught in using the protocol of the hospital."

The second paragraph brought an insight to his dismissal. Drugs, the reason he was discharged, and it was also the reason his licence to practice had been revoked.

Ah ha, this might be what I'm looking for. She repositioned the lamp. Sister Sarah carefully studied the file a second time around.

"Well the circumstantial evidence fits the picture pretty well, but that's a far piece from getting the accused to admit to the act. But it is a lead, and I intend to follow that lead wherever it takes me."

Sister Sarah punched a button on the phone.

In seconds she heard a deep voice, "This is Lieutenant Baldor. Sargent Nolan is out at the moment. Maybe I can help you?"

"This is Sister Sarah. I want to leave a message for the Sargent."

"If it has anything to do with the case here, at St. Mary's I'd like to know."

"It's just a thought, but I've scoured my list of suspects, and the only one that could fit is a doctor by the name of Jeffery. If you need his last name, I can have that for you in a day or two."

"You mean Jeffery Singline?"

"That's it. How did you know?"

"We/ve had him listed for the better part of a week"

"Well praised be your worth. I wasn't sure you knew he existed."

"Have you got time to see me? I'd like to look over the writeup. Who knows, it could be the missing link."

"I'll make time for you."

"I can be at your doorway in half an hour."

"Right now, I have a registered nurse coming for a job interview. We are short of good head nurses. Listen. I can be done with her by three o'clock. Will that work for you?"

"OK, I'll see you then."

The interview went well. Mother Superior pulled a shawl over her shoulders and called the driver: He took ten minutes, to the second, to arrive at the front of the hospital which brought him to the main entrance. Sister Sarah and her new hire piled into the rear seat. The new nurse wanted to be dropped off at the Laos depot. Sister Sarah had agreed. The trip back took 16 minutes, and by the time she walked into Lieutenant Baldor's office on the fourth floor the wall clock had struck three.

"Good afternoon Mother Superior. Has your day been going the way you would like?"

"As well as I can expect. I had excellent luck with hiring a new nurse. That was a good beginning. She will start Monday morning. Her previous experience means I can put her on the floor the day she starts. That's a joy. Help is hard to come by in this day and age."

"I'm anxious to hear what you have uncovered. We've lost a good deal of time much to my chagrin. I hope the information you have put us back on schedule. The scuttlebutt says that the parents are riled."

"I know it's slow going, but until we get that vital lead the case is at a stand still. We have everything in place. I can assure you, we are getting phone calls by the dozen, but most of them are thrill seekers trying to get their name in the papers. Hopefully, we have what we need. I made a list of every company, and every individual whether the person was a private party or a politico. I made exhaustive comparisons hoping to find someone who had sufficient motive to want a nasty revenge like this."

Baldor poured a glass of water and took a lengthy drink.

"After cross checking each and every situation pertaining to someone, who could be the person we are looking for, I came away with just one who fits all the categories. As I said before, that man was a former doctor who was employed by St. Mary's."

"I'm surprised at your diligence. Most people are not that astute. Sounds to me like I've discovered the modern day Sherlock Holmes." She returned to her desk.

"It's not what you think. I'm only doing my job as I see fit. Many people have entrusted me with their lives, with belongings, and with their safety. I'm from the old school. That simply means I value my reputation. It's what I can, and will, leave to the world. In the past several years my beliefs have eroded. But, I doubt you can find a majority to stand at my side and declare the truth of that statement. The sixties changed all that. As of now, it's far from the way our younger set views the world. And now, while the group adds years to their ages they recognize that the new scene they clamored for was light-years away. Where are the educational teachings that might have prevented the youngish drug culture from burning down the citadel of successful existence? I ask you, 'Where did all the flowers go?' For several decades the young American public brought carnage to this great land. Whether by accident or wilful intent, this nation has brutalized all attempts to neutralize the criminal element in our cities."

Her audience smiled.

"Yet year after year thousands of children are desecrated on the altar of frustration. They are in reality left to shift for themselves. Teenage mothers slip away from their duties, and if given the chance, foist the raising of the young to some caring relative. By then it might be too late, for much of how the children approach society has already become habit. What does our society do about the denial of care, where the child never finds their personal style for meeting the world?"

Her student nodded her head.

"In most cases intolerable social conditions are simply overlooked. What does one do to punish mothers who are just old enough to avoid the ravages of diaper control? Not knowing enough about the menses, they remain in fear of a death knell, a fear they feel threatens their future? What a shame, America's quality upbringing is losing out to stupidity. I suspect we can lay the blame at the feet of government. In their zeal, to shore up the educational system, they brought an end to the study of the three 'R s' It's more than pitiful. It is the 'out-of-control-burial' of good old common sense."

Baldor butted in, "You know the voting public always responds to the financial carrot that Washington throws our way every once in a while."

"Seriously, can you suggest a way to make this man confess? Of course there is the telephone. We can get a judge's permission to tap his telephone line. With legal control in hand we'll have one end of the investigation under control."

"It could be the simplest way to start getting evidence. Not knowing his telephone is being tapped, he might blab and give us what we need."

Lieutenant Baldor offered an incisive ending to the discussion, "It might give us a momentary edge. Presenting the Police with this advantage may be his downfall. Sooner or later he'll tip his hand. I do hope it's not to long."

The call came to the Police Department, early Friday. Baldor wrote down and saved every bit of the transmission. He then called St. Mary's to relay the information to the head of the hospital.

Sister Sarah answered the phone.

"Is this the Mother Superior—Sarah?"

"Yes, it is."

"Good. I have some rather suitable news. The technical branch of the department now has proof that your contention was correct. Our department began eves dropping on a call to a town just outside of London England this morning. The call was to a man named Toady who later turned out to be Jeffery Singline's brother. The dialogue included references to St. Mary's hospital, and the existing criminal intent."

"For goodness sake, that was quick. I thought it would be at least a day or two."

"The information concerning the phone call is on its way to the police here in Tucson. Once we secure the evidence in legal form, we will confront our blackmailer. There's little doubt about our trouble maker. I'm sure he will confess. Beyond that I believe we can extradite his brother as a witness for the prosecution. That would pound the last nail in the coffin."

Lieutenant Baldor's supposition was fairly correct. Jeffery confessed and produced the map that physically marked the original positions of the babies. Hearing the news the interested parents filed into the nursery and each family took possession of their individual child. The smiling faces of the relieved mothers and fathers told the true story.

Toady received a year in prison form his part in the blackmailing scheme. True to his statement, the employer severed their connection. The court, once the verdict was announced, spoke with concern.

Judge Hood lauded Mother Superior for her investigative

excellence. He further shamed the defendant, describing the act as exceeding malicious in intent. Handing down the sentence, he sternly told the jury that he could only issue the term of life in prison without parole.

"The law had not envisioned such a dastardly criminal component when the statues were written. Nothing beyond life imprisonment can be assessed."

The next day dawned. The sun appeared in brilliant color. It was a bright and cheerful day to go along with the good news. By noon the temperature reached 79 degrees. Tony and Eunice having listened to the news that everyone wanted to hear thought a celebration might be in order. A hurried call to the local liquor store brought a keg of Irish ale to the public park where the original party had taken place. Martin and Margaret donated four large pizzas, the kind with everything on them. It all came together like clockwork, and because it was the weekend, the revelry continued until near dawn. All the males in the group drank too much. The women stood back and frowned at the actions of their husbands. In light of the heartfelt relief that each family experienced, not one man received a tongue lashing from his spouse. In the fray of relief all was forgiven. The fear worn on the faces of the families involved had disappeared. It had been replaced by lighthearted gaiety. Martin looked over at his wife who was spinning around the complex congratulating every woman.

He yelled at his wife above the noise of the crowd,

"It's good to see your carefree nature again."

Margaret smiled and trotted over to her man.

"I can't believe the relief I feel. I had no suspicion that I was under such stress."

"I can see the gleam in you eye again, and that makes me happy. Sometimes men lose their way in the game of love and family. The only way I can tell everything is all right is because you light up like a Christmas tree. I'm sorry I'm not more help. I'm hoping you'll give me a rain check."

There were two other party goers who arrived via special invitation. One was Sarah, the Mother Superior, and the other person who turned up happened to be Lieutenant Baldor from the police force. That made eight couples in all.

Mother Superior, brandishing a glass of lightly colored ale, stood and addressed the group.

"Thank the Lord for his help. Solving criminal misdeeds, or solving a major crime, is not my cup of tea. I'm glad for any help I can get."

The Lieutenant raised his glass and uttered one word, "Amen."